Island of Dreams

Emily-Jane Hills Orford

To Mr. Boland

*My Grade 7 teacher, who introduced me to fantasy fiction (and many other classic genres)
and encouraged me to read Tolkien's Lord of the Rings. And so my journey began…*

Acknowledgments

First of all, I want to thank my childhood friends, teachers, family members, all those who believed in me and my passion for writing. And to those who wrote the greatest books of all time that continue to infatuate and inspire me. I'm sure I'll never run out of good reading material in any genre.

I want to thank Tell-Tale Publishing Group for believing in my stories and helping me make them available to the world to enjoy. A story is only made possible by the writers who write it and the publishers and editors who believe in it. Thanks to everyone.

Chapter One

Present

Something cold moved gently over her legs. It wasn't refreshing. Just cold. Everywhere else her body felt gritty and cold too. In contrast, something hot burned along her back. Her face was half buried. Suffocating. Where was she? Nothing made sense. Her mind moved with sluggish resistance as she tried to remember. Anything. Her memory was a void. Except for discomfort she felt only confusion. Trapped in darkness, she struggled to open her eyes.

A voice reached the auditory portion of her brain. It was a boy's voice. Young. She didn't recognize it. In fact, she was having difficulty understanding what was being said. It was loud. Too loud. She wanted to cover her ears to block the sound. Her arms wouldn't, or couldn't, move.

Help! She wanted to scream. No sound came from her throat. It, too, was gritty. Dry. It felt like sandpaper. And her eyes still wouldn't open. Or were her eyes open and she couldn't see? Was it night? She didn't know. She didn't understand. And the boy's voice kept calling. Calling.

"Father. Come here. There's a woman lying on the beach. She's not moving. And she's almost naked. Father. Come quickly. We have to help her."

Another voice. A man's. Calmer. A soothing tone. "Edouard, you know you shouldn't wander the beach alone. It isn't safe."

"But Father," the boy argued, no longer yelling. "I saw her lying here. I was looking through my telescope and saw her. No one would believe me. I had to come. She needs help."

Silence. There was a sense of someone very close, perhaps crouching beside her. She felt a light pressure on her neck. Then the voice again. The man's. "There is a pulse. A weak one. We shall get her up to Rose Cottage and Maria can see to her."

"Will you send for the doctor?"

"Yes, Edouard."

She felt something tugging underneath her body. She was gently turned, her head no longer buried.

"Her eyes are open, Father. Can she see me? Can she hear me?"

"I don't know, Edouard." A pause. "Miss. Miss." He was addressing her. All she could do was moan. At least, she thought it was a moan.

"We had best get her to the cottage. You run ahead, Edouard, and let Maria know we're coming. Then run and fetch Dr. Burns."

"Yes, Father." And the sounds of retreating footfalls were followed by the sensation of floating. The man lifted her. She could feel his arms underneath her body. Her head rolled into a firm shoulder. She felt safe there. And then the void of complete oblivion returned.

Chapter Two

Previously

"Now Aunt Olivia," Rose gently scolded the older woman walking at her side. Aunt Olivia was leaning heavily on Rose's arm. The younger woman didn't mind, but she was worried. "You must tell me when you tire. And you must take time to rest."

"I'll have plenty of time to sleep when I'm six feet under," Aunt Olivia retorted, using a line she had used frequently over the past year as death stared her daily in the face. At fifty-one, she was, or at least had been, very spry and energetic for her age. That was before the cancer diagnosis and the months of chemo zapped the energy right out of her body. This trip was something the two ladies had planned for years and it was now, finally happening. A cruise through the Caribbean. Just the two of them. On board one of the grand Royal Cruise Line's finest ships, the Royal Blue.

The flight from Toronto to Fort Lauderdale, Florida had been exhausting for them both, but especially Aunt Olivia who had only just received notice of the all-clear cancer prognosis. The oncologist had warned, though, there could be a recurrence at any time and the effects of the lengthy battle, and the heavy doses of chemo would linger for some time. Perhaps even years.

The ladies settled into the cabin. It wasn't the top floor of what appeared to be a massive floating hotel. (Not at all like the images depicted in the classic sitcoms.) Perhaps not first class, but they did have a grand room with a balcony, where they had stood for hours watching the coastline recede behind them and the splashing of crystal blue water only marred by the ships wake and the occasional pod of dolphins matching the ship's movements, stride for stride (or perhaps more appropriately, splash for splash).

They were greeted royally when boarding, since Rose, more famous for her stage name, Rosalind Melodious Bell, was an internationally acclaimed concert pianist.

"The captain wishes you to share his table for the six o'clock sitting of dinner," the steward addressed the two after showing them to their cabin. There was a large basket of fruit on the table and a huge bouquet of roses. A welcome fit for royalty.

After the appropriate thanks and the attempt at tipping, which was politely refused, "The captain's request," being the argument, the two left the unpacking and spent the next few hours on the balcony.

She attempted to entice her aunt to rest inside. Picking up the brochures on the table, Rose handed some to her aunt. "Let's sit by the window. We can study these brochures and decide what we want to see at each port of call."

Aunt Olivia took the brochures and dumped them on the side table. Walking to the window, she unlatched it and slid it open. "I plan to stand on our balcony waving to the crowds below as we pull out of the harbor. I've always wanted to do that." She motioned to Rose. "Are you going to join me?"

Reluctantly, Rose followed her aunt onto the tiny balcony. It cost considerably more to book a room with a balcony, but she wanted the best for her aunt. She wanted the dream to be real and thorough. And she wanted to share it all to its fullest. Rose didn't need to be asked twice. With a smile on her face, she followed her aunt outside, breathing in the salty air as she looked the many storeys down to the dock they had left not so long ago.

The ship's horn sounded its warning blast. The gangways had been pulled back and the line's unfastened. Slowly, with careful precision, the monstrous cruise ship pulled away from its moorings, leaving the dock full of waving crowds of humanity behind. It was a sight to behold. Cheers could be heard from the surrounding balconies and the lower decks. Everyone was in celebration mode.

"What we need is a glass of champagne," Aunt Olivia announced in a voice loud enough to be heard above the din of celebration and the repeated blasts of the ship's horn.

"Would sparkling grape juice suffice?" Rose asked.

With a resigned sigh, her aunt responded, "I suppose. Champagne would have been nice, but you're right, Rose. I must be careful what I eat and drink." She slipped an arm around her niece and pulled her close. "This is nice, though. I'm so glad you made me come." She laughed. "Not that I needed much convincing. This is something I've always wanted to do." With a final squeeze, she asked. "Shall I pour us some make-believe champagne?"

Rose shared a laugh with her aunt and followed her back into the cabin. "I'll get it. Why don't you put your feet up and we can sip our 'champagne'," she made her fingers work the magic of imitation quotation marks, "while we study the ship's rules, schedules and what we want to see at each port."

Her aunt settled into one of the deep cushioned chairs and put her feet up on the nearby ottoman. Rose poured the sparkling grape that had been left in an ice bucket on the table into the fluted glasses sitting next to it. Everything had been arranged with style and elegance, a ploy to make each passenger feel special and important. Her aunt was important and she was determined to make this trip of a lifetime be a dream come true.

Handing one of the filled glasses to Aunt Olivia, the two ladies raised their glasses, clinked them and saluted the moment. "Bon voyage," they declared to the other and took a sip.

"Mmm! Better than champagne."

Aunt Olivia chuckled softly. "And more refreshing."

Rose settled into the only other chair and placing her glass on the side table nearest her chair, she picked up a pile of brochures and started browsing the contents.

"It says here, our first stop is Puerto Rico," Rose broke the silence. Placing the brochure on her lap, she reached for her glass and took another sip of the sparkling grape juice. "There's a list of things to see. We have a couple of hours stop. What would you like to see, Aunt Olivia?" Hearing no response, the young woman looked up to find her aunt sound asleep where she sat, the brochures she'd been perusing slipping off her lap onto the floor. Thankfully the glass full of juice was sitting on the side table.

With a smile on her face, Rose replaced her glass and continued talking as if her aunt were awake and attentive. She kept her voice low, at a conversational pitch, calm and soothing. "We should explore the Castillo San Felipe del Morro. They say it's like taking a step back in time, five centuries in the past. Its location on a prominent bluff of land above the old city of San Juan, it claimed a very successful defensive position, never defeated by sea and only once overrun by land. That was in 1598. Hmmm. Fascinating." She paused to sip more of her grape juice, continuing as if she were carrying on a lively conversation. "We should also explore the old city of San Juan and take in the Catedral Metropolitana Basilica de San Juan Bautista, the second oldest cathedral in all the Americas. Oh! I'd love to see that. Wouldn't you, Aunt Olivia?"

"Hmmm!" her aunt stirred and fluttered her eyelids. "Oh! I must have dozed off. Is it time for dinner yet?"

"Soon." Rose placed the remaining brochures on the table. "Perhaps we should start preparing. I'll unpack so you can rest a bit longer."

Aunt Olivia didn't need encouragement to doze off again. An hour later, Rose gently nudged her aunt, suggesting she might want to change for dinner. The suitcases were all unpacked and tucked away in the large walk-in closet. Rose was dressed for dinner, wearing her long, formal gown, a light cotton gown that stretched down to her ankles, billowing around her legs with soothing comfort. It was light blue in color, her favorite, and was gently embellished with embroidered flowers around the neckline and down the short, puffy sleeves. A narrow band of lace outlined the V-neck. She frequently wore this dress when performing, as it was loose and comfortable, especially underneath the heat of the unforgivingly hot stage lights.

"You look lovely, dear," her aunt offered praise in a drowsy voice, muffling a series of yawns as she pushed herself slowly off the chair. "I guess I'd better make myself beautiful, too. It wouldn't do to have my niece outshine me in elegance." The ladies shared a laugh as Aunt Olivia slowly made her way to the washroom to freshen up.

The salty sea air had been revitalizing, but now, walking toward the elevator that would take them to the dining room level, Rose noticed the fatigue plaguing her aunt. She would have to curb her own desire to see and do everything so her aunt wouldn't feel the need to keep up all the time.

Chapter Three

They arrived at the dining room and were escorted across the grand space to the head table, the captain's table. Captain Smithers was standing off to the side, conversing with other passengers. Noticing Rose's arrival with her aunt, he excused himself and made his way around the table, to greet the two formally. In his crisp full-dress white uniform, with the gold braided epaulets on his shoulders and the gold buttons down the front, the slightly greying man with the deep tanned face and bright blue eyes cast a commanding figure of authority. He certainly caused the eyes of many of the ladies in the room to study him more thoroughly.

"Miss Hilton," the captain greeted Aunt Olivia first. Rose's aunt had never married, taking on the task of caring for Rose after her parents had died in a horrific accident. Rose didn't remember her parents very well. She had only been four. All she remembered were the years of Aunt Olivia's care in the rambling old farmhouse just north of Toronto, in the small, rural horse-bound community of King City. There had been horses on the farm, but not the purebreds that populated the grand estates surrounding them. It didn't matter. Horses weren't Rose's passion. She did enjoy a good hack across the fields, but she wasn't competitive by nature. At least, not where horses were concerned. She had stood out in high school, chastised for not owning the best horse in the school district, for not having the most ribbons for equestrian or dressage events. But for Rose, music was the only thing that mattered. It was her driving passion in life.

Aunt Olivia encouraged her, drove her to countless lessons, rehearsals and performances all over the Greater Toronto Area, known locally as the GTA, and beyond. Now, after years of traveling the world to perform in the greatest concert halls ever built, Rose was stepping back to care for her aunt.

Olivia Hilton was Rose's mother's, Evelyn's, younger sister. Her estate, such as it was, was known locally as Hilton Hall. It was the Hilton family homestead and had been since the early settlers claimed the land in the mid-1800s. Claimed it, cleared it, and built one of the finest horse breeding facilities in Ontario. Initially, the horses were for practical use: pulling carriages, carting cargo, and long-distance, overland treks. Sturdy horses, now the rare breed known as the Canadian horse. In the early 1900s, the Hiltons started raising thoroughbreds, racing at Woodbine and Churchill Downs, quickly establishing a stable of winners.

After Olivia's parents passed away, she and her sister, Rose's mother, managed the inheritance; but, after Evelyn's death, it was more than enough merely to keep a few horses on hand. One stablehand remained. George. Rose suspected a stronger bond between Olivia and George than just owner and hired hand, but nothing ever came of the bond. At least, not that she witnessed. George remained at Hilton Hall, allowing the ladies to venture south on the Caribbean cruise of their dreams.

"Miss Hilton," the captain repeated, taking Aunt Olivia's hands in his and giving them a warm squeeze. In spite of her harrowing experience fighting cancer, Rose's aunt was still a very attractive woman. "I am Captain Harris. Welcome aboard the Royal Blue. She's one of our newest ships. And I am honored to be her first captain. I hope you have found everything satisfactory so far?" He arched an eyebrow, expecting a response. He had yet to greet Rose.

"Everything is wonderful so far, Captain Harris," Aunt Olivia replied kindly, gently pulling her hands free from the captain's. "May I present my niece, Rosalind Bell."

Captain Harris allowed his eyes to roam from Aunt Olivia's to Rose's. "Ah yes," he smiled warmly, but not as invitingly as he had smiled at the older woman. "The world-famous pianist. Miss Bell." He gave his head a slight bow.

"Please call me Rose," the younger woman insisted. "Everyone does."

"Rose. Welcome aboard the Royal Blue. I do hope you will honor us with a performance after dinner tonight." His gaze wept with anticipation.

"I would be honored, Captain Harris." Rose returned the smile with one as void of emotion as his was. She had hoped to escape the notoriety that pursued her everywhere. She had hoped for some time away from the tiresome performance routine. But, for her aunt, she would do anything. She glanced sideways, enough to notice the sparkle of pride in Aunt Olivia's eye. No, Rose couldn't disappoint her aunt.

The captain motioned to the head table and pulled out a chair for Aunt Olivia. Once seeing her seated, he did the same for Rose. The ladies were relieved to be seated next to one another, but Rose was a little unnerved to notice Captain Harris, after motioning the others to be seated, taking a seat on the other side of Aunt Olivia. He was being a little too attentive toward her aunt. She would have to keep an eye on the two. Not that there was much she could do, as they were both adults.

Captain Harris dominated the dinner conversation. Rose had to give him credit where due. The man did manage to engage all the others seated at the head table. However, he did appear to put extra effort into conversing with Aunt Olivia.

Rose had an interesting gentleman on her opposite side. A scientist, he extolled the many mysteries of the world, including the Bermuda Triangle. Dr. McTavish, he introduced himself. No given name, just Dr. McTavish.

"Myth," he claimed adamantly. "All myth." The cruise ship would be venturing close to the Bermuda Triangle, but not too close, so Rose was interested to learn more about this mysterious enigma that appeared to make ships and aircraft vanish. "I am a man of science, my dear lady." He seemed to extoll the elegance of addressing Rose as 'my dear lady'. He all but ignored the other occupants at the head table. "A man of science. Nothing about the Bermuda Triangle has been proven. Nothing. People vanish in the ocean all the time. The simple notion of there being a geographic location that has the powers to make people disappear is ludicrous. Unscientific." He spooned another mouthful of the chocolate mousse concoction into his mouth and carried on.

"They don't call it the Devil's Triangle for nothing," the woman on the other side of the scientist muttered into a mouthful of mousse. Rose thought her name was Anna, but she wasn't sure. It was a large head table with almost two dozen people seated around it. Introductions had been made, but, as was usually the case, names were quickly forgotten once people were seated and the attention was given to those seated next to them.

"Or Hurricane Alley," someone across the table added.

"All names associated with myths," the doctor argued. "The triangle area, which is in fact quite large, is fed by a river within the ocean. We know it as the Gulf Stream. It's a major surface current, driven by thermopile circulation originating in the Gulf of Mexico and flowing through the Straits of Florida into the Atlantic. Like I said, a river within the ocean. And it can, and does, carry floating objects and moves things around with unexpected expediency."

"But planes and ships have disappeared," someone else argued. The entire table was getting wrapped up in the Bermuda Triangle discussion.

"We're not going anywhere near this area, are we captain?" Aunt Olivia voiced her concern.

"Yes, we are," Captain Harris replied. "Right through the middle of it, actually. We entered the Triangle coordinates about an hour ago. It is the most direct route to Puerto Rico. We will be moving along the edge of the Triangle area, hopefully avoiding Hurricane Helena which is headed toward Florida."

"A hurricane?" someone gasped.

"The trajectory is far north of us," the captain spoke with confidence, but his words were met with doubt and concern. "No need to worry. We may experience some rough waters, but nothing significant."

"I thought hurricane season didn't start until late autumn," someone grumbled.

"Hurricanes can occur any time of year," the doctor contributed quickly, not wanting the captain to steal his show. "It all depends on the atmospheric conditions over the northern Atlantic." He paused long enough to savor another mouthful of the mousse. "And the Bermuda Triangle myths have evolved from these same atmospheric conditions."

"I read somewhere," it was Anna again, the woman on the other side of Dr. McTavish, "that the anomalies experienced in the Bermuda Triangle are a result of leftover technology from the lost continent of Atlantis."

"Ohhh!" several voices exclaimed.

"Nonsense and rubbish," Dr. McTavish snorted, waving his spoon about to dramatize his response. "Absolutely no scientific basis for that theory."

"You claim it's all scientific," a man directly opposite the scientist argued. "Then how do you explain the planes and ships that disappeared without a trace? The *USS Cyclops*, carrying a full load of manganese ore, which went missing without a trace in 1918 along with its full crew of 309. And *USS Proteus* and *USS Nereus* which also disappeared without a trace during the Second World War. Also carrying heavy loads of metallic ore."

"Sabotage," the doctor argued.

"And the aircraft." The man wouldn't give in. He appeared to be a fountain of knowledge about the bizarre events surrounding the Bermuda Triangle. As much as Dr. McTavish was knowledgeable about the scientific aspects of the enigma. "Flight 19, a training flight of TBM Avenger torpedo bombers. They disappeared in 1945. And the search and rescue aircraft that was deployed to look for them, a PBM Mariner with thirteen men on board. They all disappeared."

"Human error," the doctor insisted.

"And wasn't there a ghost ship?" someone else chipped in. "I think it was the *Ellen Austin* that found it and placed a crew on board. Then the ghost ship disappeared with the crew, only to reappear again, minus the crew, only to be re-boarded again and then to disappear, again, along with the new crew."

"Stories," the scientist argued again. "There is no record of such an event. The *Ellen Austin* ship records show no indication of lost crew members. All stories."

"I recall reading about an incident that happened years ago." Anna used the lull in the conversation to add her contribution. "A royal yacht went missing for days and when it showed up somewhere near Puerto Rico, the only person on board was the queen. The king and his son and all the crew and attendants were missing. I don't think they ever recovered the bodies of those who were missing."

"That was back in 1919," the man who had discussed the other incidents contributed. "Exactly a hundred years ago, actually. I think it also happened in the month of June. I wonder if our trip is prophetic. After all, this is June."

Rose was more interested in the lone survivor than the theory of a possible hundred-year anniversary event. "What about the queen?" Rose asked. The story was enticing, to say the least."

"Oh, I think she lived," Anne nodded in Rose's direction, glancing around the scientist who was scowling his displeasure. "Barely. She was starving and delirious and a little mad. The stories she shared, about an island and a kidnapping and how she escaped by hiding in the yacht's kitchen cupboard, all stripped bare of food and beverages. She kept ranting about mysterious powers and magic. No one believed her. I think the king's brother, who stepped in as regent and was later crowned king after all efforts were exhausted to find the missing royals, decided to have her committed to some special care facility."

"She'd be long dead, now, I assume," Rose surmised.

Further discussion on the royal disappearance was instantly squashed. "All rubbish," Dr. McTavish declared.

Conversation was interrupted by a sudden list in the ship. She tipped precariously starboard, sending people, furnishings, dishes and food sliding across the room. Screams broke the otherwise complacent dinner gathering.

The emergency alarm sounded.

"Captain to the bridge. Captain to the bridge. All hands man the lifeboats. Lifejackets on. Please make your way to the assigned lifeboat. This is not a drill. I repeat. This is not a drill," a voice said over the speaker.

The captain had already managed to break away from the melee and slip out of the dining room to assume his duties on the bridge. Rose grabbed her aunt's arm and the two helped each other manoeuvre across the littered dining room that was tilting even more precariously.

As they made their way across the room, Rose grabbed a chair as it skittered down the sloping floor. She reached underneath and pulled out the lifejacket. She handed it to Aunt Olivia, who protested, trying to force it into Rose's arms.

"You must wear this, my dear Rose," she insisted, the trembling of nerves evident in her tone of voice. "You know my days are numbered. You have a full life ahead of you."

Rose didn't argue. She merely shoved the lifejacket back into her aunt's arms and grabbed another chair. Reaching underneath, she felt around in vain. The lifejacket had already been claimed. Several chairs later, she found an unclaimed lifejacket and pulled it free. The ladies shrugged into the devices as they continued to make a careful retreat from the dining area, which now looked like a war zone.

"We're in the Bermuda Triangle," someone muttered as they made a path through the rubble. "I wonder what the smart scientist has to say about that? Does he have a logical explanation other than scientific mumbo jumbo?"

Rose didn't hear any more. They were now on the deck, grabbing whatever they could to keep their footing. It was slippery and people were sliding past them, on their feet, on their knees, even on their backs. The cacophony of screams coupled with a vicious roar of water was washing everything clear of the ship.

The two ladies made it to a lifeboat as the ship listed more severely. The crew was scrambling to loosen the ties while those who could clambered aboard. Rose helped her aunt into the boat, hopeful that it wasn't already overcrowded. As Alice tried to climb in behind her aunt, someone grabbed her from behind and shoved her out of the way. She slipped on the deck. The last thing she remembered was her aunt's voice, screaming above the roar of the sinking ship and whatever raged around them.

"No-o-o-o-o!"

Chapter Four

Present

She woke slowly, sensing the comfort of a soft mattress and warm coverings. She could hear voices nearby. Unfamiliar. A woman's voice and a man's, the man who carried her. She wrenched her eyes open, trying to make sense of her surroundings. She wasn't sure if her eyes were open or not. Everything remained black.

"She's awake, Sir," the woman's voice moved closer.

The man's voice retreated. "I shall leave you to your charge."

The woman was close. "Can you hear me, dear? What's your name?"

"Rose," she tried to force the word to make a sound, but it came out so raspy. She felt a hand reach under her head to lift it slightly. Something cool touched her lips. Water dribbled down her chin as she struggled to make her lips part enough to allow some to sooth her dry mouth. The sound of the glass being set on a hard surface nearby accompanied the sensation of her head being lowered. She breathed deeply and tried again. "Rose." The sound was still coarse, not her usual mellow voice, but she knew she had been heard.

"Rose. Such a pretty name." The woman took Rose's hand in hers and patted it gently. "You are in Rose Cottage. So named for the marvellous collection of rose bushes surrounding my little oasis."

"Rose Cottage," Rose cackled a response. "A good place for me. For now, anyway."

No answer. Silence. The woman continued to hold her hand. "I am Maria," she finally broke the silence. "I work for the big house up the hill. But I spend my nights here. Alone. You are welcome to stay with me as long as you need."

"Thank you." She was getting control of her voice. It was softening to its more mellow tone.

"You are quite welcome," came the response. "The doctor has been to see you. For such an arduous adventure at sea, you are doing quite well. Dehydrated and starving. Another day or two might have done you in. Had not young Edouard found you lying on the beach."

"He said," Rose coughed as her voice rasped through sandpapered vocal cords. "He said I was naked. Is that true?"

Maria coughed, more a means to alleviate the strain of an awkward situation. "You were soaking wet, Rose. And the rough conditions of the salt water had ripped off most of your garments. Even the lifejacket was barely fastened. How you survived what you did, we may never know."

"Where am I?"

"Dulces Sueños Island, lass. Not far from Puerto Rico. But an island obscure from the rest of the world."

"Dulces Sueños Island. Sweet Dream Island. What does it mean?"

"Life is a dream and the quality of that dream remains in your control," Maria chuckled softly. "There I go again, trying to be a philosopher, which I'm not. Can you see me, Rose? Your eyelids are open, but the pupils appear to be focused on the ceiling."

Rose shook her head. "No. All is black. It's like it was when I was a child. All black. I'm blind again, aren't I?"

"I don't know," Maria answered. "You will have to talk to the doctor when he returns. Do you remember anything before you woke up here?"

"A ship. A boat. Aunt Olivia." She gasped and tried to force herself up. A gentle hand restrained her. "Aunt Olivia. Where's my aunt?"

"There is no one else here except you and the people of Dulces Sueños Island."

Rose let out a sob. "Aunt Olivia. Where are you?" The sobbing continued, softly, until numbness set it and she fell into a deep slumber.

Chapter Five

Time blurred. Rose slept. Awoke. Slept again. She assumed it was the second day after her rescue when Maria suggested she might like to take a bath. When her eyes opened, it was no longer intense blackness that greeted her. She could now see shadows. Perhaps her sight was returning.

"The doctor says it'll do you some good to soak and wash the remaining sand and salt off your skin." Maria was a chatterer. But it was soothing chatter. "Alicia who works up at the big house helped me when you arrived. We had to cut off the lifejacket and what remained of your clothing. Fine material, from what we could tell. You must have been wearing something formal."

"We dined at the captain's table," Rose spoke calmly. "Aunt Olivia and I."

"On board the Royal Blue. The ship's name was emblazoned on the lifejacket."

"Yes, the Royal Blue. Any word of survivors?" She asked the same question every time Maria or anyone else visited her. "Any sign of my aunt?"

"By all accounts, Rose," Maria spoke calmly, concern and care evident in her tone. "There were no survivors. The ship sank very quickly." There was something unsettling about Maria's spartan answers, something she wasn't revealing.

"But I survived," Rose argued valiantly trying to grasp onto a thread of hope that her aunt was still alive. "There must be other survivors. Aunt Olivia made it to a lifeboat. I was shoved aside and slipped off the deck into the water. That's the last thing I remember."

"There have been search and rescue teams in the area for over a month, ever since the ship sank on June 30th," Maria started to explain but Rose interrupted her.

"Past month! How long was I tossing around at sea? What is today's date? What was the date when I was discovered lying on the beach?" So many questions. So few answers. Each answer led to more questions and more confusion. In nervous agitation, she scratched her upper left arm. It was bothering her. She didn't know why. Her increased agitation seemed to intensify the discomfort.

"You shouldn't scratch," Maria scolded gently, taking hold of the offending hand and holding it firmly, but gently, to avoid further scratching. She continued, "Young Edouard found you July 31st, Rose, and you've been resting in my cabin for about a week. Today is August 8th."

"I was floating across the ocean for a month? How is that possible?"

Maria didn't answer. The silence was unsettling. Finally, "I shall lead you to the washroom and help you feel everything so you know your way around. Keep the door unlocked and call if you need my assistance. Your bath awaits." Maria led Rose into the bathroom. "Count your steps and feel along the wall so you can find your way back," she instructed. The older woman took Rose's hands and allowed her to feel the surfaces of the bathroom, so she could find everything. "I put out some clean towels and comfy clothes here," she placed Rose's hand on a pile of fabric. "The bath is full and warm. Call out if you need help. I won't be far away. Enjoy." With the parting words, Rose heard Maria slip out and close the door behind her.

The lure of a soothing bath blocked the unsettling questions mounting in Rose's mind. Was she living a dream? Or a nightmare? What and where was this place? This island? What did Maria call it? Dulces Sueños Island. Sweet Dream Island. She had to find out what was going on, what she was doing here, and where here was. And if it was real.

She scratched her arm. It was aggravatingly itching. Turning her head sideways, as if to glance over her shoulder, she whimpered in frustration, realizing again her sudden handicap: she still hadn't regained her sight. Placing the palm of her opposite hand on the irritation, she exclaimed. "What the...?" It was hot to touch. Was it a rash? A sudden vision flashed through her mind: an image of a man, leaning over her and shooting something into her arm. It felt and sounded like a staple gun. The vision faded as quickly as it flashed into her mind. She turned her head away from the irritation and shed her garments before climbing into her bath. Questions continued to flutter through her head, disappearing as quickly as they entered her consciousness.

Chapter Six

Rose didn't know how long she soaked in the bath. It felt good to wash the remaining dregs of salt and sand from her hair and body. As the water cooled, she decided it was time to relinquish the refreshing haven. She climbed out of the tub and felt around for the towel. Finding it, she dried herself. Her hair being only shoulder length would dry quickly in the warm air. She fumbled with the clean garments left out for her: a soft cotton chemise and knee length cotton shorts. She couldn't find anything for her feet, but deciding it was warm enough to go barefoot she wasn't concerned. Neither could she find a brush or a comb, so she ran her fingers through her hair and shook it loose to allow it to dry au naturelle.

Satisfied she was presentable, she fumbled for the doorknob and slowly opened it. There were voices coming from somewhere down the hall. Although she was starting to see shadows, her sight hadn't recovered, and she didn't know the layout of the house to feel her way around. She couldn't even remember how far it was to the room where she had laid recovering for who knew how many days.

She chided herself. She would have to be more observant. It wasn't as if she'd never had to feel her way through life. She had been there before, struggling to navigate the world with no vision, an ailment that was surgically corrected in her teens.

Stretching her hands in front of her, she felt around until she contacted what she assumed was the wall. One hand draping along the wall and the other stretched before her, she made her way slowly toward the sound of the voices, hoping, fervently, that there wasn't a long staircase to descend before reaching her destination. Wherever that was.

The voices became more distinct as she moved along the hall. She heard her name and paused, wanting to hear what was being said before her presence was noticed. She had so many unanswered questions. She didn't understand any of what had happened to her or where she was. Or why, for that matter.

"You have to tell her, Sir." It was Maria's voice. Who was she calling 'sir'?

"In time." A man's voice. It sounded familiar. Soft. Deep. Kind. The man who had carried her from the beach. "Only tell her what she needs to know, when she needs to know it."

"Your Majesty." Another man's voice. Further away. "You must come, now, Your Majesty. Quickly."

Rose was startled. *Your Majesty? There was royalty here?*

"Maria. I leave our Rose in your care. She will be moved to the castle as soon as possible. For safety's sake." *And a castle? Where was she? In fantasy land?* The footsteps could be heard retreating.

Satisfied Maria was alone, Rose felt her way closer to the place where she had heard the voices. "Maria," she called out, tentatively at first, not sure if she was where she should be. "Maria," she called again.

"Ah! There you are," the reassuring voice approached and Rose felt a hand on her arm. "Here, let me lead you to the kitchen. You do look better now that you've been able to wash up. I will have to find something for your feet. You will be better cared for up at the big house."

"You mean the castle?" Rose queried and was met with stunned silence. "And what did the man mean by 'Your Majesty'?"

"How much did you overhear?" Concern was evident in the older woman's voice.

"Enough," Rose answered simply. "Enough to know I have more questions than you have answers."

"How is your sight?" Maria asked.

"You're evading my questions."

"You haven't asked any yet."

"I'm seeing shadows."

"Good. That's a good sign. The doctor is confident you should have your full sight in a matter of days."

"That doesn't answer my questions."

"Then ask them."

"Where am I? What is this place? And how could I possibly survive in the open water for weeks? Without food and water?"

"Perhaps I can answer some of these questions." A man's voice came from somewhere behind Maria. Rose noticed another shadow, hovering where the light broke through a rectangular space, presumably a door to the outside world.

"Dr. Burns." Rose detected a tone of relief in Maria's voice.

"Maria," the doctor addressed the woman who had cared for Rose. "And Rose. Or, perhaps better known as Rosalind Melodious Bell, the internationally acclaimed concert pianist. It is an honor to make your acquaintance. At least now that you are in a conscious state of mind."

"Dr. Burns," Rose nodded. She scrunched her eyes, trying to evade the shadows so she could study the man closely. It didn't help. She still could only see shadows. But there was something distinctly familiar about the doctor. Scratching her arm, she had another flashback: the staple gun sound, her arm, the irritation.

"Don't scratch," the doctor scolded, in a similar tone of voice Maria had used earlier. Not waiting a response, he addressed the older woman. "Maria, perhaps we could have some nourishment. Tea and biscuits. You do make the best biscuits. I shall take Maria into the garden and you may join us there."

Was the good doctor dismissing Maria? Rose noticed the shadow approach and felt the pressure as he took her elbow. "Allow me to lead you outside. I'm sure you'll appreciate some fresh air after being laid up inside for so long."

Rose could feel the distinct change as they stepped outdoors. The fresh breeze, salty from the ocean, presumably close, washed her face gently, easing the strain that was causing her facial muscles to tighten their grip. She was tense. She knew she was. It was like walking into the limelight, on stage, somewhere significantly important like Carnegie Hall. The pressure, the tension, the need to be perfect, mirrored what she felt now: the need to know. But there was something about the air. She breathed deeply and almost instantly felt relief.

"Refreshing, isn't it?" Dr. Burns took several deep breaths of his own as they stood on the precipice, the passage between inside and out. "I never tire of the air on this island. It's rejuvenating. Healing. Stimulating."

"And confusing," Rose asked, letting out a whoosh of air in the process. "Everything about this place is confusing."

"We all felt that way at first, Rose. Most of us learn to accept and adapt. Most of us; sadly, not all of us." There was a tone of melancholy in the last few words, but the doctor quickly carried on. "Let's sit in the garden to the left." He led Maria, commenting on various steps and obstacles along the way, until he was able to position her in front of a garden seat or bench, Rose didn't know which. "Sit." Dr. Burns sat, gently tugging Rose's arm so she sat beside him.

"Honeysuckle?" she queried. "I think I smell honeysuckle. My favorite. Is it August? That's what Maria said."

"Yes. Everyone can smell their favorites in this place. As for the month? I'm really not sure. Time here is very ethereal, to say the least. When was the last date you recall?"

Rose wondered how time could be ethereal and why everything seemed so strange here. Then she pondered briefly. How long had she been here? That fateful night on the cruise ship. The last time she saw her aunt. "June. I know it was June. Dr. McTavish was regaling us as we shared dinner at the Captain's table. He was talking about his scientific theories regarding the Bermuda Triangle while others at the table were sharing stories they had heard, people who had disappeared in the triangle. Someone said it was exactly a hundred years ago to the day that some royal family went missing. That happened in June 1919. Only the queen and the royal yacht were recovered."

"She lived, I understand," Dr. Burns commented, melancholy again evident in his voice. "Yes, things do seem to happen in June." He was silent for some time. The breeze continued to sooth. "Rose," he broke the silence tentatively. "I'm not sure I'm the one to tell you this, but His Majesty is otherwise occupied at the moment."

Rose interrupted. "There you go, now. Calling someone *His Majesty.* Who is this *Majesty* person?" She gave her head a slight shake and noticed her vision clearing, the shadows becoming more distinct shapes. And colors. "My eyes," she exclaimed, her hands reaching her cheeks as she took in the sights around her. It was all coming back. "Oh my!" her previous questions were forgotten as she took in the vast array of colors that stretched as far as the horizon.

The doctor sat quietly next to her, allowing the young woman to relish in her returning eyesight. "All it took was a little time," he murmured.

The excitement dimming, Rose turned to the man seated next to him and studied him closely. Seated, he looked to be about her height. His eyes were a bright blue and the slightly graying temples enveloped a kind face, one with crease marks that suggested both age and wisdom. She broke the silence. "How old are you?" she asked bluntly.

He laughed softly. "You are studying me closely. How old do you think I am?"

Now it was Rose's turn to laugh. It was a nervous laugh, more like a chuckle to ease the tension she felt inside her. "Mid to late forties."

Dr. Burns didn't respond immediately. He looked deeply off into the distant, well aware that Rose continued to study him. Finally, he answered. "In your perspective of measure years, I am

145 years old. I was born 1874. I trained in medicine in Edinburgh before following my calling to serve king and country. I was on that fateful royal yacht in 1919. As was His Majesty and his son, the boy who found you. His Majesty is King Frederick III of Luthenstein, a country that no longer exists due to the Second World War which annihilated so many small European countries. But, in 1919, Luthenstein was one of the wealthiest, most influential and prominent, yet small, countries in the world."

"And his son?"

"Crown Prince Edouard. He would have made a fine king, following his father's example, to defend the country through the many trials and conflicts of the twentieth century."

"But the prince is merely a lad of what? Ten years of age?"

"Yes," the doctor nodded, stealing a quick glance at the young woman beside him. "He was only two when the yacht encountered a ferocious storm and we all woke up on this island. We were as confused as you are now. There were people, hundreds of them, who had found this haven long before we did. They helped us adjust. Only Queen Eleanor never did adjust. She stole away one night, presumably aboard the yacht, and managed to escape. According to all accounts we received from beyond, she lived a short life following her rescue, in an institution. Everyone listening to her stories about this place believed her to be insane. The king's nephew took the throne and the country suffered greatly. Then came the wars."

"In 1919, Europe was still recovering from the First World War." Rose had never been strong in history, but she knew enough. "How was it that Luthenstein was so rich and powerful at such a time of flux?"

Another chuckle from the doctor. "King Frederick was clever. He played both sides well and stayed out of the conflict. The country prospered during the First World War."

"I'm still very confused. You don't age on this island. You can't leave or you become insane. What is the purpose of this place? And where is it?"

Dr. Burns let out a deep sigh. He was about to respond when another man's voice intervened. "I think you've told her enough, Doctor." It was the man who had rescued her. The king. His Majesty.

Rose glanced in the direction of the voice and studied the man standing mere steps away, framed in an arch of climbing roses in full bloom. The posing created a regal effect, suiting the royal figure. It also captured a flutter in the young woman's throat. She blinked rapidly, steadying her sudden case of nerves. Dr. Burns had already jumped to his feet and greeted the man with due honor, "Your Majesty." Rose was about to stand up as well, but the king motioned for her to remain seated.

"You may leave us, Doctor."

"Yes, Your Majesty."

"Thank you, Dr. Burns," Rose called out. The doctor merely gave her a quick nod then made a hasty exit down the garden path in the opposite direction from where the king stood.

"It is good to see you up and about, regaining your strength," King Frederick spoke clearly as he took the few steps necessary to approach the bench where Rose sat. Taking the doctor's place, he leaned somewhat forward, head tilted to face the young woman. "The doctor means well. He told you quite a lot about this island. Perhaps too much."

"Not enough, really," Rose intervened, cautiously, not sure how to address this man, this royal personage sitting so close to her on the bench. "I still have so many questions."

"About Dulces Sueños Island?"

"Yes. And about its inhabitants and why we are all here."

"We have been chosen, Rose. May I call you Rose?" She nodded and he continued, "Quite simply, we have been chosen.

For our gifts, for our desire to see the world as a better place than it is now. To repopulate the world once the end finishes."

"The end?" Rose was even more confused than before, but now she was also frightened.

"You must have seen the signs. Heard the warnings. The damaging storms, raging fires, horrendous wars. The world is dying. In fact, it may already be dead beyond recovery. That is, the world as we both knew it in our respective times."

"And we will create a better world? One full of the perfect humans, hand picked by some unknown entity? Isn't that rather presumptuous? Selective breeding, in a way?"

The king laughed. A deep, hearty laugh that sent ripples up the young woman's arms and down her spine. Seeing a look of shock on Rose's face, he cleared his throat. "I'm sorry. I shouldn't laugh. But you misunderstand. We have a wide range of chosen people – some with autism, Down's Syndrome, PTSD. You name it, it's all here. The chosen people are those who had something positive to contribute to the new world. The chosen people are those who offer no threat to this new world's well being."

"For how long?"

"Forever."

"And what about animals, wildlife, natural vegetation?"

"All chosen, selected and cared for until such time as we reach out to re-populate the planet."

"A real Noah's Ark."

"You could say that."

"And why me? What's my gift to this new world? You say we were chosen, but what choice did we have?"

"Given a choice, who would choose to die? You were chosen for your music, for one," the king finally tore his eyes from the young woman he had been studying so intently. "And your beautiful inner self."

"For what purpose?"

He slapped the palms of his hands on his knees and stood up. Walking toward the arch through which he had entered earlier, he added, "Some things you will have to find out on your own. Over time."

"Is the world about to end?" she called out in despair, not wanting to think about a world she loved and cherished being gone for good. "What about my aunt? My friends?"

"All gone." The voice echoed back from the receding figure of the king. Rose was left alone in the garden to think over all she had just learned and the many questions that continued to multiply inside her head.

Chapter Seven

Maria appeared at Rose's side as the younger woman watched the receding figure of the king. "I'll take you up to the big house now," she said softly.

"Is it a big house? Or a castle?" Rose asked casually, not really caring about the answer. She had enough answers to know that things were getting stranger by the minute, and she had no way of controlling it.

"I suppose it's more of a castle, than a big house," Maria responded. She took Rose's arm gently, but the young woman shook it off.

"I can see, now, Maria." She glanced at the older woman and gave her a half smile, not sure whether she felt like smiling given what she was learning about this place and her situation. "But tell me, first. How old are you?"

"About the same age as the doctor," was the simple answer. "And, yes, I came over with the royal family on the yacht to care for the infant Prince Edouard. He doesn't need my care now, so I have other things to do."

"Like care for bodies washed ashore?" The answer was a soft chuckle.

The women made their way slowly along the path that meandered away from Maria's cottage. There was a slight rise in the land and the exertion of climbing started to wear on Rose. She paused at a bend that snaked around to climb more steeply. Looking back the way they had come, Rose marveled at the beauty of the landscape: the gardens, the wooded areas, the colors and, in the distance, the ocean. She breathed deeply, taking in again the rejuvenating calm of the saltwater breeze.

"It's beautiful here, Maria."

The older woman paused next to Rose. "Yes, it is. I never grow tired of the view. Or the air. So clean. So fresh."

"I don't think I've ever smelled fresh air like this before," Rose declared, stealing another deep breath, and then exhaling slowly.

"You probably haven't," Maria agreed. "There is no pollution in our little Garden of Eden."

"Is that what this is?" Rose glanced at the older woman, studying her in a way she hadn't previously, since she had only recently recovered her eyesight. Like Dr. Burns, Maria appeared to be in her late forties, with the faint lines on her face and the slightly graying hairline to prove it. She was about the same height as Rose, so the younger woman could look Maria directly into the eyes – deep blue eyes, like the doctor's. "Does everyone here have blue eyes?" she blurted out.

Maria merely laughed in response. "Perhaps. You shall see for yourself soon enough." She gently touched Rose's elbow. "Come along," she urged. "We're almost there. We'll get you settled into your rooms and then you may rest. I'm sure all this exertion, so soon after your ordeal, must be exhausting."

Rose merely nodded and turned to follow Maria up what she hoped was the final rise in the path. It was. They reached the top and emerged through another arch of prolific roses into a large open green space. Rose gasped. "It really is a castle! Does Cinderella live here?"

The older woman laughed again. "I love your sense of humor. As for Cinderella? Perhaps she's just moving in."

"I'm no Cinderella," Rose parried in response. "More like a sanderella since I was washed ashore onto a sandy beach and arrived covered in sand."

More laughter as the older woman walked across the green, her young charge keeping pace, eyes glued on the destination.

"You might want to close your mouth," Maria whispered in a teasing tone of voice. "You'll only catch more flies."

Rose snapped her mouth shut. "Ugh! There's flies here?"

"Of course. There's something of everything here."

They approached what appeared to be the rear of the castle. Rose couldn't be sure, not having seen the front, but she assumed that, since Maria was employed by the Crown, so to speak, then she would be required to enter through servants' entrances only. Rose didn't know where she fit in. Perhaps she was to be indentured as a servant, too. Though she wasn't sure what good she'd be as a servant. She couldn't cook or clean at the best of times. Her life had always circled around music. And Aunt Olivia.

The thought of her aunt brought on a sharp pang of loneliness. How she missed her. She spent years travelling the world on her own, but in the past they had only been a phone call away. Now, even the phone connection had been severed. It left a hollow feeling in the pit of her stomach. A void that would never be filled.

The ladies entered a hallway. It took a few minutes for Rose's eyes to adjust to the dim lighting after being outside in the bright sun. Once her eyes were focused, she studied her surroundings. Finely polished wood panelling lined the walls, adorned with portraits of what appeared to be royal personages. Long tables stretched along the walls, displaying fine pieces of china, silver and sculpted busts and small sculptures. A lush rug woven in reds and blues stretched the length and felt soft against Rose's bare feet.

Maria suddenly noticed the younger woman's feet. "I should have found you something for your feet," she gasped. "That was short sited of me. And yet you managed the uphill walk from the cottage in bare feet." She glanced at Rose's face. "Amazing."

Rose smiled. "I hadn't noticed until now. Not really. But this carpet is very soft and comforting to my soles."

"We shall find footwear in your rooms," Maria continued, walking more briskly. "And a complete wardrobe as well. You will find everything you need. And, if not, all you have to do is ask."

"If everywhere is as soft as this carpet and the ground outside, do I really need shoes?" Rose chuckled softly. She was starting to feel more like herself. It startled her. Everything was happening so quickly.

She felt an itch on her upper left arm. Automatically, she reached with her opposite hand to scratch. The itch didn't ease. In fact, the scratch sent sharp shivers up her arm and across her shoulders before descending along the spine. Startled, she yelped and stopped in her tracks. Looking at the source of irritation, her eyes bulged as she took in the raw, red spot that enveloped a raised patch of skin. "What the…?" She didn't finish the exclamation. "Maria. What is this? What have they done to me? What have you done to me?"

Maria hesitated before turning back. "We all have them, Rose," her voice was a vain attempt to sooth. It didn't.

"Maria. You have to explain. Please. What is going on?" Agitation shuddered through the young woman's body, her eyes widening with fear. "What is this?" She pointed to the irritation.

"It's where they implanted the nanorobots. We all have them." She raised her sleeve and showed a scar that matched the raised patch on Rose's arm. "It keeps us well. Strong. Young. It's what's healed you so quickly."

"Robots!" Rose added. "It turns us all into robots. But why? And I'm not healed. Not really. It's all an illusion. This is all an illusion. Why? Why? Why?" She was screaming, now, her fingers viciously scratching the irritation in a vain attempt to remove the electronic devices from her boy.

Maria gently grasped Rose's hand. She held firm, even as the younger woman resisted. "It's all for a purpose. The king will explain. Later. For now, we must get you settled. And into more suitable attire."

"More suitable for what?" Rose continued to resist, not as effectively as she would have liked. Maria held her hand firm and pulled her along the hall toward a grand set of stairs.

"Come along. Your room is at the top of the stairs. Just beyond the master suites where the king rests. And not far from the young prince's set of rooms. You will be more comfortable once you're settled and rested."

It was as if something inside her was taking over. The nanorobots? All resistance evaporated and Rose followed where she was led with complete complacency. As if there was nothing out of the ordinary happening to her or around her. Something niggled at the back of her mind; something that suggested all was not right. The irritation eased, but only slightly, and the thought of nanorobots pouring through her veins dimmed to a trickle. Was it Maria's touch that sparked a surge of energy from the older woman's nanorobots to the newly implanted ones inside Rose?

"I have allergies, Maria," Rose muttered as she stumbled up the stairs. "If these nanorobots are made of metal alloys or organic material, I'm probably reacting to them." Her words were starting to slur, but she had to force them out.

Maria settled Rose into a grand set of rooms. She hadn't taken the time to study the layout or the décor, only focussing on the inviting canopied bed. Maria tucked her in, Rose obligingly cooperating. All thoughts evaded her consciousness as she slipped into oblivion. Darkness engulfed her. She heard voices around her, but she couldn't respond.

"They're irritated." A woman's voice. "She has allergies."

"We didn't know." A man's voice.

"How could you not know? How could they not know? The rash is spreading. She was becoming delusional. She could have gone into anaphylactic shock. Then what would you have done? What would they have done?"

"The nanorobots are doing their job. Keeping her alive."

"And poisoning her at the same time. She's allergic to something in their makeup. If we don't remove the nanorobots, she could die."

"We'll have to suction the blood from her veins and remove the nanorobots."

"It'll kill her."

"They won't let that happen."

"Who? The nanorobots? Or them?"

The voices dissipated into a vacuum, echoing and ricocheting across the distance as if rattling around in a massive black hole.

Chapter Eight

The fog inside the vacuum lifted. Slowly. The voices had long since disappeared. She could barely remember what was said. Nanorobots. Tiny technological wizards. Robots. Draining her blood. Where was she? In Romania? Bran Castle? Dracula's castle?

She wanted to shake her head to clear the cobwebs. Instead, she dragged open her eyelids and blinked rapidly as the bright lights of the space around her blinded the pain. She groaned.

"She's coming around." The woman's voice. From a distance. Perhaps the other side of the room. She wasn't alone after all.

Fingers touched her forehead and she felt one eyelid lifted and a bright light flashing back and forth. The action was repeated with the other eyelid. The light hurt. She groaned again and tried to wrench her head free of the intrusion. Her hands lay like lead at her sides.

"Rose. Can you hear me?" Dr. Burns was calling her. "She has good corneal reflexes. She appears to be conscious. Or, at least, she's starting to come around."

"Rose," Maria's voice emanated from the opposite side of her head. It was close, but soft. Soothing.

Rose opened her eyes again. The blinding glare wasn't so bad this time. She blinked and managed to keep her eyelids raised long enough to see the shadows of the two figures who spoke. "Where am I?" Her voice croaked, barely audible.

"Give her some water," the doctor instructed.

Rose felt a hand behind her head, gently lifting it and a straw being strategically placed between her lips. She sucked in the refreshing liquid. The sandpaper feeling inside her mouth became saturated. She tried to speak again. "What happened?" She coughed. The straw was reinserted. Again, she drank. "Where am I?" Her voice was gaining more sustenance. She didn't cough this time.

"You are in the castle, Rose," Maria spoke. "A guest of His Majesty, King Frederick III of Luthenstein, now known as King Frederick I of Dulces Sueños, soon to be King Frederick I of Novae Terrae."

"Novae Terrae?" Rose croaked a response. "Where's Novae Terrae?"

"The world as you know it, Rose," the doctor took over the conversation. "That world is no more. Armageddon, the Day of Judgement from the New Testament, has happened and the new order must take over."

"What?" Rose exclaimed. She was fully conscious now. She attempted to push herself into a sitting position, failing miserably in her weakened state. "How can that be?"

"Natural disasters relating to climate change and human carelessness. Senseless wars. It was bound to happen sooner or later," Maria pointed out.

"I listened to the doomsday reports for years. No one believed them. The world was supposed to end in the year 1000, in the year 2000, and so many other set dates over the centuries. What happened this time?" The nanorobots in her system were doing their job. Rose's voice had returned and her mind was working diligently and effectively. She was fully conscious. The figures, previously fuzzy, were clear. She recognized Maria standing on the left side of her bed and Dr. Burns hovering over her right side. She noticed them cast conspiratorial glances at one another. "You have to tell me," she insisted.

Taking a deep breath, Dr. Burns proceeded. "It's a lot to explain, Rose. And a lot to take in. The storm that capsized your cruise ship was much more than another tropical storm, or even a hurricane for that matter. The waves that enveloped the ship tore into the coastal communities and literally washed them away, buildings, vehicles, people – everything and everyone in its path. It swept across the North and South American continents, picking up momentum and destructive power that magnified significantly once it reached the Pacific Ocean. It then swept across the ocean, tearing apart islands along the way until it reached Asia." His voice caught in his throat. "It was all over in a matter of hours, Rose. The world is gone."

"But how is it that I survived? And this place? Everything and everyone here survived. How? Why?" She shook her head in disbelief. "I can't believe Armageddon happened everywhere else but here. I can't imagine it happened at all."

"It has happened, Rose." Maria reached for the younger woman's hand and took it gently in hers. It was a soothing motion, calming.

Dr. Burns didn't wait for more questions. Instead, he provided a spartan explanation that began with a question. "You've heard of the Bermuda Triangle?"

Rose nodded. "During dinner at the Captain's table, Dr. McTavish was arguing about the scientific aspects of the geographic area known as the Bermuda Triangle. Others were discussing the myths and legends surrounding it."

"Ah yes! Dr. McTavish." The doctor spoke as if he knew the man. "He was here, you know. On Dulces Sueños Island. The largest and most central island within what you know as the Bermuda Triangle. He arrived about the same time as the queen. When she escaped, as she claimed she had to do, Dr. McTavish followed her example. Many years later, I might add."

"Really?" Rose was surprised. "So, this is the Bermuda Triangle. It's what saved me." She shook her head as if to clear the cobwebs from her mind. This was all very confusing and making little sense, if any. "But, if he were here, wouldn't he believe in its existence?"

The doctor cleared his throat before continuing. "I know you still have lots of questions, Rose. For now, know that you are safe.

I can see the nanorobots we replaced in your system are working efficiently in restoring your health, without the allergic reaction you experienced earlier. I apologize for the scare resulting from the first batch. We don't often have allergic reactions to this technology. You were the first one. But, as the great bard wrote: "All's well that ends well". The king will fill you in on the remaining details which should answer the rest of your questions. Perhaps, Maria, we should allow the young lady some time alone."

Maria nodded in agreement. "I laid out some clothes," she instructed. "And you have your own private bathroom. Look around and get to know your space. Dinner will be in about an hour. The king and the prince look forward to having you join them this evening. You have much to discuss."

Rose was about to ask more questions, but the two made a hasty departure,

Chapter Nine

Alone, Rose slid her legs over the side of the bed. Sitting up caused the room to spin. Or so it felt. She blinked. Once. Twice. The spinning slowed, then stopped. Were the nanorobots helping her adjust? Making her heal quickly? She didn't know if she really was healing quickly, as she didn't know how long she'd been out. Or, for that matter, what they'd done. The last words she remembered were a man's voice, probably Dr. Burns, saying they'd have to drain her blood. Is that what they did? She'd have to ask. It seemed rather extreme, but what did she know about these things? Not much, obviously. Everything about this new existence was one big question mark.

She glanced around the room. It was large, much larger than even the finest hotel rooms she had used on her travels. And it was elaborately decorated, deep blue damask covered the walls, set off against the pristine white corniced ceiling which framed Rococo style frescoes, theatrically illustrating reclining figures of women and muses, mostly small animals. The door through which Maria and Dr. Burns had exited was heavily paneled with a beautifully carved cornice door frame. As she glanced around, she noticed the other doors were similarly constricted.

A marble fireplace dominated the far wall, with a grand portrait of some female royal personage hanging over a mantle. A pretty clock sat, centered, underneath the portrait, the clock encased in a marble urn with an elegant lady standing next to it. The soothing ticking echoed throughout the room.

Rose stood up slowly. Her bare feet sank into the plush carpet of purples and golds that stretched the length and width of the room. The nightgown she wore trailed her ankles, its soft cotton texture so familiar to her, like a favorite she wore often when lounging around her home. She ran her hands gingerly downward. It couldn't be the same one, could it? She shook her head at the thought. Stealing her mind away from the comforts she once enjoyed, she walked around the bed, trailing one hand on the tapestries, in predominantly green and purple with gold braided fringes, that hung from a canopy, draped from a central point which appeared to be a gold crown. The tapestries stretched to the four corner posts before dropping its length to the floor, overhanging the embroidered fabric panel that wrapped around the base of the bed.

All Rose could do was gape at the heavy crown on top, centered dramatically at the peak of the canopy. "I wouldn't want that thing dropping on me in the middle of the night," she muttered to herself.

She walked slowly around the room, marvelling at the furnishings, the commodes and chests that held clothing and other personal items, the tables that sat against the walls, all made of finely polished wood with sculpted decoration including fleurettes, seashells and foliage, all richly decorated with gilded bronze.

She made her way to the alcove of large picture windows, an inviting bench filling the space underneath the windows. She kneeled on the embroidered cushion and leaned toward the center window, through which bright streams of sunlight sparkled. Fumbling with the crank, she managed to open the window, allowing the fresh air to flush against her face.

"Mmm!" she breathed deeply, allowing her eyes to close gently to feel the complete rush of the cooling breeze. "How can the world be gone and this place exist?" Once again, she was talking to herself, in whispers as if afraid someone might hear her speak.

Leaning across the window ledge, she studied the landscape that spread out before her. Fields of wheat and other crops stretched as far as the eye could see. Livestock dotted various pastures. Horses neighed and galloped around their enclosure. It was very pastoral. In the distance, tall mountains pointed steeply to the sky, providing a natural barrier between the land, the sea beyond, and the people who cared for both. She could barely see the water, presumably the ocean, through a narrow break in the mountain range, but she distinctly smelled the salt in the air. Paradise? It was almost too good to be true. And how could this place survive the Armageddon that had, as Dr. Burns explained, destroyed the rest of the world? Or was it all just a fabricated story to make her feel relieved to be alive, to be here?

She slid back from the window and, pulling up her legs, settled into the window seat. Without thinking of her actions, she reached for the doll sitting in the corner. "Anna," she whispered, hugging the doll close to her chest. It certainly looked and felt like her treasured favorite doll from childhood. Holding it away from her, she studied it closely. The dress was like the one Aunt Olivia made for the doll years ago when the original clothes became torn and ratty. She shook her head. No. It couldn't be.

Putting the doll aside, she reached for the book that lay in the same corner. "Black Beauty", her childhood favorite. The worn edges gave it the appearance of being loved and well read. It, like the doll, appeared similar to the one she kept in her home near Peggy's Cove, Nova Scotia. Although she had been brought up in King City, once her music career was launched, Rose had established herself as the resident musician at Dalhousie University in Halifax, choosing to live outside of town, within an hour's drive. The coastal community was ideal and her tiny cottage allowed her space to relax and unwind after performances and teaching at the university.

Picking up the book, she ran a finger fondly along its spine before opening the cover. She read aloud the inscription she knew she'd find, "To Rose, Merry Christmas, 1992 Love Aunt Olivia." It was her book. It was her doll. But how?

She set the book down on the window seat next to the doll and stood up, taking in the contents of the room more thoroughly.

A large bookshelf, loaded with books, lined the wall next to the window. Rose pulled out another favorite book, "Jane Eyre". It was a first edition, very valuable. Just like the one she owned, the one she had cherished all her growing up years, the one that had been in her family for generations. This one was hers. It had to be. Hidden proof was the piece of paper that slipped out from between the pages as she carefully opened it. A love letter she had written years ago, but had never sent. Her first crush, really, a passion she felt for a cherished teacher, one she later discovered was homosexual and would probably have laughed at her advances. She had been only sixteen at the time. The letter had been tucked inside the book she was reading, this one, and forgotten, sort of. She knew it was there, but it wasn't something she sought, merely something she kept as a reminder of an early feeling. She had only felt love a couple of times over the years, nothing overly serious. Her music had been her passion, all consuming, dominating her life and her soul.

She replaced the letter and tucked the book into the shelf, allowing her hand to fondly trace the spines of the other favorites neatly shelved. Tears leaked from the corners of her eyes. These books were hers. How and why, she couldn't explain. More questions that needed answers.

The clock on the mantel over the fireplace chimed four times. She should bathe and dress for the evening. Perhaps it would be a time to get more answers to the mounting list of questions. Glancing at the clock on the mantel, her eyes scanned the other items lined up on either side. Photographs. She walked closer. Gasped. Her photographs. Her first piano recital at the age of five, Aunt Olivia standing next to her at the piano. Her parents wedding photo and another one with her parents holding her as a baby. The photos had sat on her dresser all through her growing up years in King City and as an adult living in Nova Scotia. And they were here. She shook her head in disbelief. How was this all possible?

Walking over to the door Maria had indicated led to the wardrobe, she pulled it open. A light shone inside revealing racks of clothing, neatly hung or folded on shelves. Two women bustled around. Startled by Rose's sudden appearance, they graced a little curtsy and offered apologies.

"We're still unpacking your things, Miss," the younger of the two volunteered. "It only arrived this morning, so there's lots to unpack."

"My things?" Rose queried, making her way to the nearest rack. She pulled out a dress she remembered wearing to her last performance in Toronto. How long ago was that? A month? Two months? Time was a blur and all that had happened since the cruise ship was like a black hole of nothingness. "How did these things get here?"

"They were rescued before the tidal wave struck Nova Scotia," Maria spoke from another doorway tucked away in the corner, presumably the entrance used by staff who cared for the wardrobe.

"You knew about the disaster before it struck?" Rose gasped. "Couldn't you have saved more people?"

"We saved as many people as we could and as many treasures as well," Maria explained simply.

"So, there is a way out of this 'Bermuda Triangle' phenomenon?" It was more of a question than a statement.

"Yes. But only for those with the ability and desire to return," Maria said. "Your piano sits in the music room on the main floor. It suffered minimal damage which can be easily repaired, or so I've been told. Such a beautiful instrument."

"My piano? Here?" Rose gasped. The baby grand Heintzman, early twentieth century, had been in the family since it was purchased from Heintzman's in Toronto in 1910. Aunt Olivia had laid claim to it as a child, followed by Rose's mother and then Rose. It hadn't moved from the King City homestead until Rose established herself in Halifax. She couldn't part with the cherished instrument, with the soft, melodic tone and the treasured memories of hours spent tinkling the ivories, so to speak. And now it was here?

"Perhaps you'll play something tonight," Maria suggested.

"I haven't played for so long," Rose bemoaned. She couldn't remember the last time she played a piano. Any piano. The captain had asked her to perform after dinner, but that was before the ship capsized and everyone drowned. How long ago was that?

"You may surprise yourself." Maria was not to be put off. "With your talent, anything is possible." The older woman pulled a long gown from the end of the rack. "I think you should wear this for dinner tonight."

"I thought you had already laid out my wardrobe for this evening," Rose challenged. She didn't mean to snap, but she was frustrated with all the questions that kept mounting. She wanted to know – everything.

"I think this one is better." Maria handed it to Rose. The long silky gown felt like it melted on the younger woman's outstretched arms. Red with delicate flowers intricately embroidered, the dress had been an impulse purchase months ago while performing in Italy. She hadn't worn it yet. Tonight would be the first.

Nodding, she turned to make her way back into the bedroom. She draped the dress over the end of the bed before heading to the bathroom. Her confusion was mounting, but the questions would have to wait till later.

Chapter Ten

An hour later, Maria knocked on Rose's door. When the younger woman answered, Maria greeted her with a smile and said, "You look lovely. I'll lead you downstairs. His Majesty is waiting in the drawing room along with his son and Dr. Burns, of course. I believe young Prince Edouard is anxious to meet you, now that you have fully recovered."

"He saved my life," Rose responded with a nod. "I don't know how he noticed me on a beach so far from the castle and went to my rescue. I can barely see the ocean from my window."

Maria chuckled. "There are checkpoints and watchtowers all around the castle. Young Prince Edouard is very curious and loves to visit the watchtowers. He spends hours scanning the open waters through their telephotopic equipment."

"Telephotopic?" Rose queried. "I've never heard that term before."

"It's a type of telescope," Maria gave a brief explanation. "I'm not very technically minded, so it'd be best to ask the experts. If you're interested."

"I'm beginning to realize that there's a lot around here that needs explaining," the younger woman muttered. They had reached the top of the stairs. Maria glanced over her shoulder briefly before leading the descent.

Voices could be heard as the ladies reached the bottom step. Maria veered off to the right with Rose close behind, following the trail of men talking. The older woman pushed back the panelled pocket doors, the grinding creek of the motion putting a stop to the conversation as the ladies' presence was announced. The doors opened like a stage curtain being drawn back and the light from the room beyond engulfed the hallway like a stage spotlight, its central focal beam enveloping Rose. She felt the surge of energy that trickled through her veins every time she walked onstage to perform. This was no different. Not really.

Head high, Rose followed Maria into the drawing room. As the older woman stepped aside, Rose continued walking until she was a few steps from the man she had conversed with in the garden. Was it earlier today? Or days ago? She didn't know. It didn't matter. Or did it?

With a slight tilt of her head, she managed a graceful curtsey and said, "Your Majesty."

A young boy's voice interrupted her formal greeting. "It's her, isn't it Father? The one I found on the beach. The one who..."

"Edouard." The king's stern voice shut down the rest of the young prince's spoken thoughts. What was he about to say? Was there more to this than a mere rescue?

Rose turned her attention to the young boy standing next to the king. "And you must be Prince Edouard, my knight in shining armor." She flashed her warmest smile and was rewarded with one in return.

Glancing up at his father, the boy spoke in a rather loud whisper, "She's pretty, isn't she Father?"

Rose felt a blush creep up her cheeks and warmth pouring through her veins. The king didn't answer. He coughed. A nervous cough.

"Yes. Well," he stuttered. "All formalities aside, I believe you know everyone here. So, perhaps I can offer you something to drink while we await the call for dinner. What can I get you?"

"Just a glass of water would be nice," Rose answered softly, her nervous system having taken a jolt from the boy's comments. Her mouth was suddenly dry making water a better choice than alcohol.

A butler, if that's what he was, was instantly beside Rose, handing her a glass of crystal-clear water, complete with ice cubes and a slice of lemon. "Thank you," she acknowledged the man, somewhat startled at his ability to appear almost as soon as she had put in her request.

The king pointed to the plush, cushioned chairs that wrapped partially around the glowing hearth. The day had been warm, but the chill of evening was settling in and the gentle blaze added just enough warmth.

"I believe you have quite a few questions, Rose." He took a seat facing Rose. Maria sat next to her, the doctor on the other side with Edouard curled up on the floor, looking quite comfortable sitting cross-legged. "But before we address your questions, perhaps it would be best to set our formalities aside. When it is merely the four of us in this room, then please call me Fred. I find Frederick too formal and Freddie too childish. After over a hundred years of being a king in limbo, so to speak, far from my throne and domain, I need some modicum of familiarity amongst friends. And I would like to add you, Rose, to my list of friends."

"Me, too," Edouard piped up from where he sat. He shut his mouth sharply after a quick glance at his father.

"Very well, Fred," Rose responded in a soft voice. "And what about you, young Prince Edouard."

"Edouard, please," the boy beamed at being asked. "I like being called Edouard. It is, after all, my name." Everyone chuckled at the boy's response.

"Then Edouard it is," Rose gave him a warm smile. "Now, perhaps we can address my questions. First and foremost, what is this place? And why has it not suffered the same demise which, I've been told, has recently destroyed the rest of the world?"

The king paused, studying Rose intently. "Where do I begin?"

"At the beginning, Father," Edouard prodded. He shot a pleading glance at his father before allowing his gaze to catch Rose's eyes. Her eyes were darting around, too, though mostly focused on the king sitting opposite her.

"Well, then," he cleared his throat, cast a quick glance at the hearth, then back at Rose. "It is a long story. Perhaps we could start before dinner and finish after dinner. I must request that you keep all your questions until the end, because some of the story will answer your questions. Bear with me." He cleared his throat again and forced a half smile. "Thousands of years ago, people from another world, another planet settled on our planet. Settled on Earth. They thought they had found the oasis they sought, the ideal home to establish their New World. Novae Terrae. They built a fine community with a large city on an island in the Aegean Sea off the coast of the Attica region of present day (or more correctly what once was) Greece. Near Athens. They named their island Atlas, and the city was called…"

"Atlantis," Edouard interjected, excitement and enthusiasm mixed in the tone of his voice.

"Edouard," the king gently scolded his son.

"Sorry, Father."

Rose spoke up before the king could continue. "But the stories of Atlantis are all myths. Plato wrote about an ideal state. His story has Athens repelling Atlantis and the deities, the Greek gods showing disfavor toward Atlantis which then sinks into the Aegean Sea and disappears into the Atlantic Ocean."

"Not myths, my dear Rose," Fred's gaze latched onto Rose's as he continued. "Legends. Plato wrote about legends, based on fact. The fabled Atlantis did sink in the sea and float away to the ocean. But it didn't disappear from earth. The mere fact that Atlantis could float away suggested that the island on which it sat was more than just a natural geological island of rock and stone. It was what remained of the space craft that transported these people to earth. A space craft far advanced even in our current time. The Atlanteans, as the Greeks referred to them in legends, allowed their craft and the island they created to float until it settled in the center of the Atlantic Ocean, expanding its power and dominion. And there it sat, for thousands of years. To wait. For mankind to catch up. Which it almost did. And it might have done so, had mankind not taken upon itself to destroy the planet in the process of advancement. And destroy each other as well."

"The Bermuda Triangle," Rose gasped. "That's one of the many theories about the Bermuda Triangle. That it's the buried city of Atlantis."

"And so it is," Fred nodded. "Though not really buried."

"Are these people, these Atlanteans, still around?"

"Very much so. They are the ones who saved your life. Twice. First with the nanorobots that your body reacted to so severely and secondly with the newer, non-allergenic nanorobots that erased the symptoms that were putting you into anaphylactic shock. You will meet them soon. But they wanted me," he waved his hands to indicate the others gathered, "actually all of us, to help you settle in and understand things better before actually meeting you in person."

A knock on the door interrupted the story. A man stood on the threshold. "Dinner is served, Your Majesty."

"We should continue this over dinner." The king stood. Holding out his arm, Rose, having stood as well, took it and allowed him to lead her out of the drawing room and along the hall to the dining room, where a long table was set with fine china and silver. The room, like the drawing room, was brightly lit with candelabra and candles and a welcoming hearth blazing at the far end of the room.

The king led Rose to the far end of the table before taking his place at the head. Rose stood by a chair at the king's right side, while Edouard stood on the opposite side. Maria and Dr. Burns took their places, Maria next to Rose and Dr. Burns next to Edouard. The butler who had announced dinner and led the parade to the dining room, pulled out the king's chair, while other liveried men did the same for the others. It was all very formal — pomp and circumstance and all that. Rose wasn't accustomed to such formality. Meals, to her, had always been a necessity, a time for quick nourishment before addressing the next task on her busy agenda.

As Rose settled into her seat, she glanced down the long stretch of empty table, half expecting others to suddenly appear and take their places. The table was set at each place, as if others were expected.

Fred, as she was beginning to accept the king's less formal name, noticed her glance. "There will be others tomorrow. Everyone wants to meet and welcome our new member of the community. We had hoped to have everyone here tonight. Dr. Burns suggested a smaller gathering for your first evening. Especially since you've only just regained full consciousness. Though the nanorobots do their healing work rather fast. I agreed with Dr. Burns. Plenty of time to meet the others as well as the Atlanteans."

"But we're all Atlanteans now, aren't we Father?" Edouard queried. "Socrates says we are."

"Socrates? The Socrates?" Rose gasped, her eyebrows lifting to accentuate her surprise.

Everyone nodded in unison.

"He must be thousands of years old," she exclaimed.

"He is," Dr. Burns chuckled. "But don't tell him that. He's rather sensitive of his age. We all are." The others joined in the doctor's laughter.

Rose merely sat, looking stunned. "How many people live on Dulces Sueños Island? Where and when did they come from? Were they chosen? And why?"

She was met with an uncomfortable pall of silence. She was beginning to think many of her questions would go unanswered.

The king broke the silence. "At last count, 25,001."

Rose blinked in response. "25,001. Am I to presume that my addition to the community topped the population of 25,000?"

Dr. Burns cleared his throat. "Actually. No. There was a birth last night. A boy. The parents were supposed to join us this evening, but the baby arrived earlier than expected and changed their plans. We thought you might like to welcome the newest addition and meet his parents. One of us will take you tomorrow."

Forgetting her other questions, Rose squirmed uncomfortably in her seat. "Why? I'm not very good around babies. Or children, for that matter. Is there a reason for me to meet his parents?"

"Yes," the others spoke in unison. Even Edouard. With eyes averted, they busied themselves, fumbling with the napkins.

Further discussion was avoided with the arrival of servants carrying bowls of steaming broth. When a bowl was placed in front of her, Rose sniffed deeply, allowing the alluring steam to drift to her nostrils. "Clam chowder?" she half queried, half exclaimed.

"I understand it's one of your favorite dishes," Fred spoke.

"It is, but how did you know?" Once again, no answer.

"We have lots of clams," Edouard piped up, breaking the stunned silence. "Sometimes I help harvest them."

Rose gave the boy a warm smile. "I bet you're very good at it. I used to harvest clams near where I lived in Nova Scotia. It's more fun than work."

The boy nodded eagerly in agreement. "Perhaps I can take you sometime."

"I'd like that." The others were avoiding conversation, dipping their spoons into the chowder and sipping it with care. She followed suit. The warm, thick, creamy concoction melted in her mouth and, for a brief respite, she savored the chowder and nothing else.

When the bowls were emptied and carried away, she picked up the conversation with a request. "How about finishing the story of Atlantis?" she suggested.

"Dr. Burns," Fred glanced across the table. "Perhaps you could pick up the story where I left off."

The servers had taken away the empty soup bowls, replacing them with plates of steamed white fish, boiled potatoes, sliced cucumbers. A covered basket of bread was set in front of the king, who instantly reached for it. Flipping back the cloth, he pulled out a chunk of brown bread that emitted its own steam and delicious aroma. "The fish is sole," he explained as he passed the basket to Rose. "We have a number of freshwater hatcheries where we preserve and cultivate the various fish species from around the world. I understand sole is also one of your favorites."

"It is. Thank you for being so observant and considerate," the young woman responded.

"Dr. Burns," Fred verbally nudged the doctor.

"Yes. Well. I think you recall our king here," he cleared his throat, "Fred, that is, regaling how the Atlanteans were from another planet. Far across the solar system in a distant galaxy. From my studies of their past, I learned how their ancestors destroyed the home planet, Atlantea, through greed, misuse, pollution, wars, all the things humans have done on planet Earth over the centuries. A group of Atlanteans, mostly scientists, came together and combined their knowledge to create a means to escape, to live long enough to start another home for Atlanteans on another planet."

"The nanorobots," Rose half muttered as she took a bite of the fresh bread and savored its warmth and spongy texture.

"Yes. With nanorobot technology, they could, quite literally, live forever. It kept them young, or at least slowed down the aging process and could potentially keep them at a desired age forever. The main thing is that these nanorobots kept them healthy and strong." All the time the doctor talked, he was meticulously spearing the sole on his plate with a fish fork and gingerly placing a morsel into his mouth where, as sole often does, it dissolved with such ease that there really wasn't a break in his monologue. "Mmm. This sole is delicious. As always. My compliments to the chef."

The butler ducked his head in response and noted with clipped formality, "I shall inform the chef, sir."

"Yes. Please do." The doctor took another mouthful before continuing. "Basically, these Atlanteans were, are, a very technologically advanced society. However, like all living creatures, their people were competitive. Greed was ripe and the lure of power a seductive weapon. Technology became the tool that eventually destroyed their world. Quite literally. It imploded, like the art of demolishing a high-rise skyscraper. As far as our Atlanteans know, they are the only survivors. They searched the galaxy seeking a planet to call home. They had high hopes for this planet. They sought a locale in the Mediterranean, initially, connecting with the tribes of Israel. You've probably read of the people in the Bible who lived into their hundreds. Adam was what? 930 years. Noah was 950 years. Abraham was 175 years old. His son, Isaac, was 180 years. Some Biblical scholars argued that the length of the year was measured differently than it is now. Perhaps. However, the Atlanteans claim they had implanted nanorobots in the bloodstream of some of the Israelites. Those they believed were of greater value in the well-being and nourishment of the community as a whole."

Having finished her sole and potatoes, Rose placed her utensils properly on the plate to indicate that she was done. "So, the Atlnteans think nothing of selective breeding," she argued.

"It's not really *selective breeding*," Dr. Burns pointed out. "They weren't choosing who was born. More like who was allowed a longer, healthier life for the betterment of the world. For the preservation of world peace and prosperity."

"Sounds to me like these Atlanteans like to play God," Rose countered, not convinced all was well with this Atlantean situation. The servers removed the plates, replacing it with another main course, consisting of a thick slice of tender roast beef, lathered with a thick brown gravy and a side of beans, green and yellow, slick with the butter that it was tossed in. "Oh my!" she exclaimed. "Quite the feast. I hope I can do it justice."

"Plenty more where it came from," the king noted, picking up his utensils and starting to slice into the meat.

Returning her attention to the doctor, Rose continued with her argument. "From what little I have seen and learned while here on the island, this is definitely a situation where people are selected. Chosen. Isn't that rather presumptuous and discriminatory. What about the billions of people swept away from the destructive tsunamis that ripped the continents apart? Didn't they deserve to be chosen, too?"

"You are missing the point, completely." The doctor's voice revealed his frustration.

"I don't think so," the young woman countered.

"Oh, but you are." Dr. Burns carefully placed his utensils on the plate, not in the manner that suggested he was finished, but, rather, crossing so it proved he was still enjoying his meal. "My dear. We all go through life choosing and making selections. Do you not go into the grocery store and choose one apple over another? Or you choose chicken instead of turkey? Do people hiring workers not choose one worker over another? Do you not choose to perform one piece of music instead of another?"

"It's not the same," she pouted. Feeling full, she placed her utensils on the side of her plate. She couldn't eat another morsel.

"Isn't it?"

"Why are Rose and the doctor arguing?" Edouard broke the tension with a simple question. "I make choices all the time," he added his tidbit to the conversation. "And when dessert is served, I'm going to select chocolate over all the other choices. Does that make me a bad person?"

Rose relaxed her face. The muscles had tensed as she argued, as they often did. She gave the young boy a reassuring smile. "I'm sorry, Edouard. I guess I did get a little carried away. There is so much I don't understand and so many questions that still need answers."

"And you shall have them," the king spoke before Dr. Burns could add any more spice to the stew he had brewed. He cast a look his way, before taking up the story. "The Atlanteans recognized in the humans of Earth a similar pattern of self destruction to the one that had annihilated their own world. They hoped to avert a similar course here. When they realized they couldn't stop the process that began even in the beginning of human history, they made adaptations to their plan to save not only their own people, but also the people of Earth."

"But it's still a very selective process." Even as she spoke her words, Rose knew that her argument was falling flat. She didn't feel comfortable with the idea of being chosen. Of being selected. "I can understand why so many others were selected, I suppose. They must have met some criteria in mathematical or scientific brilliance. But why me? I'm merely a musician."

Maria cleared her throat and took her turn with the conversation. "But we need music and all the arts. Besides," She gave a demure smile. "Amadeus specifically requested you."

"Me?" Maria nodded in response. "Amadeus as in Mozart?" The older woman nodded again. "But why?"

"He's been following your recordings and performances of his piano sonatas," Dr. Burns interjected. "And he's composed more than the thirty-two you know of."

"Really! When do I get to meet him? I can't believe I'm actually going to meet Mozart. In person. Wow!" She shook her head in disbelief, unable to fathom the miraculous idea of meeting people from across the centuries. She was stunned. There were no other words to describe what she was feeling. She stared at her hands, resting on either side of the place setting, which now hosted a dessert plate and a crystal bowl of pudding topped with fresh berries. She wasn't sure she could eat another mouthful of anything, but the concoction looked delicious, as did the tray of pastries placed in the center of their end of the table.

Edouard broke through her ponderings. Speaking with his mouth full and another spoonful of pudding and berries making its way to his mouth, he said, "Try some. It's really yummy." Spoken like a true youngster. At heart, any way. Rose had no way of knowing how old he really was?

Gingerly picking up the spoon set on the side of the dessert plate, Rose scooped up some pudding and berries and slowly brought it to her mouth. She wasn't consciously considering her actions, her mind still a fog of information, most of which was unbelievable at best. The dessert made contact with her taste buds and she couldn't resist uttering a sound of pleasure. "Mmm!" she exclaimed. She beamed across at the boy. "Yes. Very tasty indeed."

He appeared pleased with her response. "Father says you might perform for us after dinner," Edouard continued his dialogue of idle chitchat. "I want to hear you play on your special piano. Your Heintzman. It's such a pretty instrument."

"I understand it was in the family for years," Maria added, also slowly consuming her dessert. "Tell us about it."

Rose sat back and pondered, trying to decide where to start. "My great grandparents purchased the piano around 1901. With its unique wood carving trim, and the fact that it's slightly larger than a baby grand, though not as large as a concert grand, it's believed that the piano sat on display in the Heintzman main store for years before my family acquired it. No one wanted something so big and so unusual for their living rooms. Even though it was a beautiful piece of furniture. So, the instrument may have been built in the 1880s or 1890s. We really don't know. But it has been cherished with each generation. There was always someone sitting at the piano, but I guess I was the only one who took music seriously enough to make it into a career. I do love that piano, even though I have performed on some pretty amazing pianos around the world. My family's Heintzman is a real treasure." She paused, allowing her eyes to connect with one person after another, finally resting on the king's. "I still can't believe you moved it here. Why? How did you know the end was near? How did you know I would be here?"

Chapter Eleven

Rose lay on the bed, fully clothed, allowing the darkness to envelope her surroundings as she reflected on the evening's events. She hadn't received all the answers she wanted, many of her questions being met with a startling void of silence. However, she had been reunited with her beloved piano. After dinner, the king led the way to the conservatory at the rear of the castle. It was overwhelming. Not just the luscious selection of plants, but the instruments that spread out across the huge expanse of space, all underneath a glass come. As she entered, she gaped upwards and all around, taking it all in as her feet tapped on the mosaic tiled floor. There was too much to assimilate all at once. She almost missed the centerpiece of the room. Her piano. Perched on a step above the rest of the room, it was the focal point to anyone entering.

After running her hands gingerly over its surface, allowing her fingers to ripple across the keys, she had taken a seat on the special stool that was as much a work of art as the instrument itself. And she had played. As she had never played before. As if she hadn't been away from her instrument for months. The music seeped into her soul and erased all else. She didn't register the audience, her dinner mates and others who had snuck into the conservatory to hear her play. When she finally finished playing – Beethoven, Mozart, Debussy and so many other favorites – she was surprised at the thunderous applause that rewarded her performance. There had been tears in her eyes as she glanced around the crowded room. Unable to take it all in, she had slipped off the stool and scurried to the nearest exit to make her escape. It took some time, but she finally found her way back to her rooms. No one stopped her.

A knock on the door made her glance toward the intrusion. "Rose. It's me. Maria. I just want to make sure you're okay."

She took a moment to answer, then spoke quietly. "I'm fine, Maria. Just tired."

"Can I get you anything?"

"No. I'm fine. Thank you."

"Sleep well, then."

Alone again, Rose allowed her eyes to roam the space around her, now cast in deep shadows. A distant rumble rattled through the air. Thunder. A flash caused her to jump. She glanced out the window in time to witness another flash light up the sky, followed by another rumble of thunder. Then the rain started. Slow, at first, then heavier until it sounded like a herd of wild buffalos charging through the castle. It was a good analogy even if she had never really seen a herd of wild buffalos charging anywhere, let alone through a castle. And it made her wonder if this sacred island, this oasis that had the 'best' of everything and every living creature – she wondered if there was a herd of wild buffalos on the island.

As the rain transitioned into a steady drone, a rhythmic cadence of percussive sounds, the young woman's eyelids drooped and she was lulled into a deep, dreamless sleep.

For the first time in a long time, Rose woke up feeling rested. Refreshed. She had left the windows open, welcoming the gentle breeze as it swept the space around her, soothing and cleansing all at once. Even her home in Nova Scotia hadn't provided such a luxury. At least, not in recent years. The polluted salt waters of the ocean swept dead fish to the beaches nearby, drenching the air in an unfathomable stench. Rotting fish wasn't the only smell that permeated what once was a popular seaside resort attracting tourists by the thousands every year. The wildlife that lived by the water dwindled, meeting the same fate as the fish. Rotting flesh was everywhere. But so was the horrific smell of oil, poured onto the beaches from leaking tankers and offshore oil wells. No one bothered with safety measures. No one cared to clean up the spills.

And then there was the plastic. Bottles and bags littered the ground between Rose's doorstep and the waters. She cleaned away the mess on a daily basis, when she was home. She diligently tucked the plastic into blue bags and blue bins, leaving it at the curb for the weekly garbage pickup, only to watch with disdain as the truck dumped her contributions into the back and then bounced off to the next house down the road, miscellaneous plastic jittering off the back of the truck as it moved along. In despair, she had started carting the plastic collection to the depot, the back of her car picking up the stench of saltwater, oil and dead fish, anything the plastic had been exposed to. She wondered if her efforts were all in vain. Even if it did make it to the recycle depot, would it end up in the landfill? Or, back in the ocean? She sincerely doubted the plastic was properly recycled.

Fresh air was definitely something to cherish. And protect.

As she savored the luxury of waking up slowly, she breathed deeply, allowing the fresh air to soak her lungs. It felt good. She stretched and pushed herself into a sitting position. Not only was the air seeping into her room, but the bright sunlight as well. If this wasn't paradise, she didn't know what it was. But she felt a deep need to find out.

Slipping her legs over the side of the bed, her feet felt the warmth of the plush carpet. Her shoes were discarded at the end of the bed. The clothes she had worn the previous night, and slept in, were wrinkled and twisted around her body. Shaking her head, she stifled another yawn before standing and making her way to the window. It wasn't a good habit, sleeping in one's clothes. Not the most comfortable way to sleep.

Leaning over the window ledge, she poked her head through the open window. No screens. Did that mean no bugs? That would be a plus. After years of living next to a polluted shoreline where flies abounded, she wouldn't miss the bugs for a minute. As if on cue, sadly, a buzz met her ear and flew over her head and into the room behind her.

"Ugh!" she groaned. "I guess even paradise needs its bug population." Ignoring the annoying insect, she allowed her eyes to roam across the scene that she had savored for the first time the previous day. All seemed well, the vegetation sparkling with both dew and the rain that had fallen overnight. It made the world at her doorstep look fresh and clean.

With another deep breath, she ducked back into her room and made way to the bathroom to freshen up for the day ahead. After a quick wash, she discarded the formal attire and pulled on her favorite sweat suit, thinking again how wonderful it was that so many of her personal items had been carted to this mysterious island. Picking up her sandals, she shuffled barefoot to the door. She poked her head into the hall, not wanting to disturb anyone. It was quiet. Almost too quiet. As if she were the only person in the entire castle. Was she?

She didn't pause to think about it. Her goal was to make her way to the conservatory, if she could find it again, and pour her heart and soul into a good solid stint of practising on her treasured piano. It was the only way to start a day. At least, that was her opinion.

Chapter Twelve

Allowing her sandals to dangle from one finger, she wiggled her toes in the thick, plush carpet. She probably could have worn her sandals and made little or no noise at all. She didn't want to chance it. She tiptoed across the hall and down the grand staircase, her feet sinking into the thick floor covering with each footstep taken.

She was surprised that she found the conservatory with ease. Her sense of direction had never been good at the best of times. As she tiptoed into the room and pulled the door closed behind her, she let out a deep breath, one she hadn't realized she was holding. She paused on the threshold. The enormity of the silence enveloped her, compressing her sense of safety and well being.

Why is it so quiet? Shouldn't there be someone moving about at this time in the morning? Where are all the castle staff? Didn't they have chores to do?

Something wasn't right. She trembled, unsure what to do next. Should she continue with her plan to practise, to play on her piano? Or, should she scout out the others and find out what was really going on?

She took another tentative step into the conservatory. The polished floor felt cool against her bare feet. No sound. She felt like she was inside a black hole, with all her possessions and the world spinning around her. She took another step, then another, until she found herself standing next to the piano. Her piano. She ran a hand gingerly over the finely polished wood. The world might be closing in around her, but her music would set her free. It always did.

Putting down her sandals, she slid her feet into them, knowing the solid soles were better for pedalling than bare feet. She sat at the keyboard and allowed her fingers to rest on the keys, briefly, before running the fingers up and down its length, performing one scale after another. The sound of the instrument broke the emptiness of the space and the silence that engulfed her dissipated as her fingers moved from scales to chords to arpeggios and then she launched into a riotous interpretation of Mozart's Alla Turca movement of his A-major piano sonata. Working through the complicated chords and arpeggios, she played every repeat, ending with the resounding repetitive A-major chord, the tonic chord, with great finesse.

Pulling her hands off the keyboard, she placed them on her lap, listening intently as the music dwindled away and died in the far reaches of the conservatory. She was winded. Music did that to her. She breathed deeply, cocooned in her little world of music and silence.

As the final echoes of the music dissipated and her breathing leveled, a thunderous round of applause accompanied with riotous "Bravos", erupted the space, making the young woman jump. The clapping approached, along with footsteps. The interloper, there was only one, surprisingly since the applause sounded louder than one pair of hands, came to stand next to the piano, glancing down at the seated musician, his hands continuing its rapturous applause.

Rose gasped. "Amadeus Mozart!" she exclaimed.

"My dear," he spoke in clipped English, his native German evident in the accent. "I'm not sure I imagined this piece being performed with such bravado. But well done! I do applaud your performance. As I have every other performance you have given over the years." Noticing her look of surprise, he continued, "Yes, I had the means to listen to you perform. And it was always breathtaking. You do my music proud, Rosalind Melodious Bell." He waved a hand dramatically in front of his face as if emphasizing his point, or swishing away accolades.

"I have always loved your music, Maestro Mozart," Rose expressed with pleasure. "And please call me Rose." She studied the man who approached the piano. He must be over 250 years old and yet he looked no older than the thirty-five years of age that history recorded when he died in 1791. The long, curly hair still sported the deep brown hues of a young man and, tied back as it was, placing him in the era of the late eighteenth-century. Yet, here he was, standing next to her piano, talking to her as if they were old friends, comrades in their shared love of music. "Especially your piano sonatas."

"And you must call me Amadeus," the great composer insisted. "I have been around long enough to realize formalities are not worth the time nor the effort. Now, about my music, I do hope you will consider performing some of my newer sonatas, the ones I composed here after I supposedly died. My original thirty-two sonatas really don't do my musical excellence and abilities justice."

"How many more have you composed?" Rose asked.

"Hundreds." The man had turned away and was walking toward a large, glass-encased cabinet next to the door to the main part of the castle. Opening the cabinet, he pulled out a sheaf of paper and returned to the piano, shuffling through the lot as he moved. "Here," he selected a small bundle and handed it to Rose. "I have performed my own work, but it needs a new set of eyes. And, I want your eyes to do the honor."

Rose accepted the papers and placed them on the music stand, lining them up so they were in the order indicated by the measure numbers marked at the beginning of each line of music. She was too focused to notice Amadeus walk around the piano and come to stand on her left side, looking over her shoulder, preparing to turn pages as needed. Nor, did she notice others entering the conservatory and taking seats to become an audience to her performance. It was her and the music. Nothing more. "Piano Sonata 367," she half-whispered the title, "in F major by Amadeus Mozart, 2004." She studied the notes and allowed her fingers to randomly work through some of the passages. It was clearly Mozart's work. It was his style. She could definitely sight-read and perform this new work with ease.

Without glancing up, she launched into the opening lines, a dramatic accolade of chords identifying the key of F major. It was a slow opening, Largo, much like the first movement of Beethoven's Sonata in F minor, the ever-so popular and difficult Appassionata. Only Beethoven's work was in a minor key. This work by Mozart was in a major key and distinctly more passionate than Beethoven's early nineteenth-century work. The Largo transitioned into a very powerful, forward driven Allegro.

Rose performed every repeat, allowing her emotions to follow the line of melody and the power of the harmony that drove the music forward. She played through the five movements with ease. Five movements in Mozart's time would have been an anomaly, the norm being either three or four movements for a classic sonata. The first movement transgressed into a slow Adagio, an elegant display of primal passion. The third movement was a slow Minuet and Trio, basic ternary form. The fourth was Allegro, followed by the very explosive Vivace final movement. She was more than winded when she played the final chords. Mozart had maintained the basic Classical forms in his composition, but the centuries of listening to and studying the works of others had definitely influenced him.

The round of applause that greeted Rose's finale was overwhelming. "Bravo. Bravo." Even Mozart's voice was heard next to her ear as the rest of the room exploded in accolades.

As the sounds of an appreciative audience dwindled, Amadeus gathered the sheets of music off the stand. "I am so pleased to have you here, Rose. You and I will make a great team in preparing the music for the future. Life anywhere and anytime cannot survive without music. As my dear friend, Friedrich

Nietzsche once said, *without music, life would be a mistake.* Between us, we shall make sure that life never is without music."

"An ominous task, to be sure." She pondered the maestro's words carefully. "And now, I suppose you're going to tell me that the German philosopher, whose words you quoted so eloquently, is also with us on this island?" It was half a question, half statement, presented with a raised eyebrow of curiosity.

Amadeus cleared his throat. "But of course, my dear. Surely you didn't think our new world could exist without one of the greatest minds of all time. Not only was he a philosopher, he was also a composer, art critic, poet, philologist and a Latin and Greek scholar. We need him here. We need him now and well into the future."

"Philologist?" Rose queried the one term she didn't recognize.

"An historian who studies and analyzes both written texts and oral historical sources," the maestro replied. "That's perhaps the simplest definition. In short, he knows a lot about the past and how to improve our world for now and for the future. And, he understands the importance of music."

With a nod of vague understanding, Rose allowed the topic to drop. The German philosopher was just another great person on her 'to meet' list, which appeared to be growing by the minute.

People were congregating around the piano, compressing her space. It was somewhat claustrophobic, but she was relieved to discover a few familiar, friendly faces in the group. She glanced across the piano and met the king's eyes.

"I'm surprised to see so many people in the audience." She couldn't think of anything else to say. Feeling unsettled, she continued with her observations. "The castle was totally empty when I awoke and came down here to practice. Where was everyone?"

The king cleared his throat and allowed his eyes to dart around the space separating him from the young woman seated at the piano. "I believe you will learn soon. That and so much more." He shuffled restlessly. "Suffice it to say that we had a community meeting of sorts and everyone was expected to attend."

"Everyone except me," Rose retorted.

"All in good time, my dear," Amadeus was the one to console Rose. "All in good time."

"All in good time," the king agreed. "Now. You've been up for some time. Have you eaten?" Noticing Rose's slight shake of the head, he continued, "I believe breakfast is the first order of business. After you've eaten, the good doctor plans to take you to meet the newest member of our community."

"Then we all go to visit the Atlanteans," Edouard piped up from where he had been standing so quietly next to his father. "And, can you teach me to play like that?"

Rose chuckled softly as the others favored the boy with a smile. The king patted his son on the shoulder. "Well, young man," Rose responded. "I can certainly teach you how to play the piano. The rest is up to you. And you'll have to practice lots."

The boy groaned. "That sounds like a lot of work."

This time, everyone laughed heartily. Rose spoke up. "It is, Edouard. Everything worth doing requires work."

Edouard uttered another groan, accompanied by a facial grimace.

Chapter Thirteen

Several hours later, after a satisfying breakfast of oatmeal and toast, accompanied by bacon and eggs, Rose accompanied Dr. Burns as they left the castle and crossed the wide expanse of well tended lawns and gardens.

"I still don't understand why I should meet a little newborn baby," Rose broke the silence that had engulfed the pair as they exited the castle grounds. "What does this baby have to do with me?"

"You shall see," the doctor answered with a continued sense of vague commentary. "Maria is already there, helping with the care of the infant. She always did enjoy working with newborns."

"You like Maria, don't you?" Rose couldn't help but notice the flush that spread up the doctor's neck and across his cheeks. "If you care so much, why not tell her? Why not pursue your interest?"

The doctor merely cleared his throat, something Rose was starting to recognize as one of the doctor's nervous habits. He didn't say anything else, merely walking at a brisker pace. Rose had to trot slightly to keep up with him. She breathed a sigh of relief when he suddenly slowed down as they approached a quaint, thatched roof cottage in the middle of a grove alive with blossoming fruit trees and all kinds of wildflowers and wild herbs. The aroma that accosted Rose's senses was bordering on being narcotic in its hypnotic effect. And the steady drone of pollinators engulfed her auditory senses.

"Here we are," the doctor announced. He called out in a loud voice to announce their approach. "Hello, there."

In response, a figure appeared at the door. Raising a hand in greeting, the doctor responded in kind. The figure, a man, left the cottage and approached. He was tall, lean and tanned from hours spent in the sun. As they came closer, Rose couldn't help but feel a sense of recognition. She had met this man before. She racked her brain, trying to secure the memory.

"James," Dr. Burns greeted the man. "And how fares the newes addition to the Bell family?"

Bell. James Bell. "Daddy!" Rose exclaimed, using the pet name she had used as a child. Her hands flew to her cheeks which were flaming with a flushed sense of disbelief. She hadn't seen her parents in decades. Other than the photos that sat on her shelf, she had pretty much forgotten what they looked like. And yt, here was her father. "It can't be. It's not possible."

"Rose." The man walked toward her, ignoring the doctor. "My little Rose. You have grown into a fine young woman."

"Daddy. Dad. Is it really you? But how? I thought you were dead. In an accident." Rose knew she was muttering a confusing list of random thoughts.

"Yes, my Rose." James reached for his daughter's hands and took them in his own, allowing his eyes to search Rose's. "Our boat capsized and we were washed ashore here. I don't know what happened to the boat, but we have been here ever since."

"The boat was discovered just off the coast of Florida," Rose explained. "Or so Aunt Olivia told me years later when I was old enough to understand. Old enough to ask the questions." She shook her head in disbelief. "But why didn't you let me know? At least you could have done that, couldn't you?"

James shook his head, a note of sadness evident in his eyes. "No, Rose. I couldn't. Once here, we had to stay. And wait."

"Wait for what?"

"Wait for you." He let loose a deep sigh. "Your mother is inside. Anxious to see her little girl again. We did keep up with your growing up years and your successes as a concert pianist. We couldn't be more proud of our little girl."

"But you weren't there for me." She couldn't keep the sharpness from her voice. She was upset, saddened by all those lost years when she could have enjoyed her parents' presence through it all. Tears leaked out of the corners of her eyes and dribbled down her cheeks unchecked.

"No," James sounded as sad as Rose felt. "We weren't there for you. But we are now. And, you have a little brother to meet."

Rose stepped back suddenly. She was shocked. "I have a brother? The newborn baby Dr. Burns mentioned is my brother? And that's why it was so important for me to meet him? What do I want with a brother now when I didn't even have a family all those years ago when I needed one?"

She was angry. She bit her tongue, trying to curb further hurtful comments. It didn't help. The sadness and the anger crept in anyway. James stepped forward slowly and wrapped his arms around the young woman. At first, she resisted. Then, as if the years of missing her parents were washed away, she leaned into him and sobbed quietly on his shoulder. As he patted her back gently, he said, "You have a family now. And Aunt Olivia did a good job as your family."

Rose cried. She cried for the family she lost as a four-year-old. She cried for the family, for Aunt Olivia, whom she lost only weeks ago. And she cried for the family that had resurfaced, strangers in so many ways.

Finally, the tears abated. Pushing away from her father, she wiped the corners of her eyes with the heels of her hands. "Here," her father handed her a linen handkerchief. She took it and sniffled as she wiped her face dry. She moved to hand it back to him, but he shook his head. "Keep it." She nodded and tucked it away. "Now. Let's go see your mother and meet your baby brother."

He held out his hand and Rose took it. No reluctance. Once again, she was a four-year-old trying to understand why her parents had to go away.

"But why, Daddy?" she had asked as they took one last walk around the stables behind Aunt Olivia's house. The horses knickered a welcome, but the two walked on, oblivious to all the world except each other.

"We're scientists, my little Rose," Daddy tried to explain. "Your mother and I are extremely concerned about the fate of the oceans. World pollution is exploding at an alarming rate. The icebergs are melting. And…" He was about to say more, but stopped abruptly, remembering that he was talking to a young child. His daughter. He didn't want to scare her.

"It's a research voyage, my little Rose." He always called her his little Rose. "You wouldn't have anyone to play with. No pets. No horses."

"I could play the piano." Rose had recently demonstrated an interest in music and the family heirloom that graced Aunt Olivia's house. The family stayed there when not traveling on research trips. Sometimes Rose was allowed to tag along, but mostly, like this time, she was sheltered with her aunt while her parents went away to do their research.

"Sadly, there is no piano on the boat." Her father gave her a mournful look.

"You could put it on the boat, couldn't you Daddy?"

"Not this time, little Rose. There's no room with all the research equipment. Perhaps on our next trip. As a family."

They returned to the house. Rose's mother had finished packing and the luggage was in the front hall waiting to be loaded into the taxi when it arrived. The taxi would take them to the airport in Mississauga and from there they would fly far, far away.

The memory faded as Rose stepped into the cottage and heard the unmistakeable wail of a newborn.

Chapter Fourteen

Rose really didn't know what to expect. She hadn't seen her parents in almost thirty years. Everything that had happened to her since waking up on this island had been questionable at best. Now this. Her parents. Alive. After all these years of believing them dead. Had Aunt Olivia known? She didn't think so. More questions. And questions about questions. Would she ever have full disclosure?

The cottage was small, compact, but neat. She followed her father, if that's who he was, and she was inclined to believe he was, into the main room. There was no front hall or foyer. The front door opened into the large room, presumably a sitting room given the cluster of comfortable chairs surrounding a stone-walled fireplace with a thick wood mantle. Photographs covered every horizontal surface and paintings pixelated the wall space. Mostly landscapes. Impressionistic. She would study them later.

The room was dim, the only light seeping through the large bay window next to the front door and a smaller window over a bookcase next to the fireplace. The room was, quite simply, cozy. Homey.

The doctor's voice could be heard somewhere toward the rear of the cottage. Rose's father was making his way toward the sound. She followed in his footsteps. A narrow hall led past a tiny, but serviceable kitchen with closed doors opposite, presumably the bedrooms. The lighting was more restricted in this narrow space, lined with bookcases overflowing with books of all sizes and description. The door at the far end of the hall was ajar, emitting a thin stream of light. The voices appeared to be coming from within that room.

Dr. Burns was scolding his patient. "You may get up and walk around." His voice wasn't loud, but it was authoritative. "But only short walks. Inside. Nothing too exertive. You had a difficult birth and you don't want to rush things."

"Moving around is good," a woman's voice argued. The sound of her voice pinged a gentle memory deep in the recesses of Rose's mind. It was her mother. It had to be. But how? "I can't lie around all day doing nothing."

The doctor chuckled softly. "I hardly think caring for a newborn would be classified as doing nothing. And, I agree. Walking and moving is good to restore circulation and promote healing. However, all in moderation. At least for a few days. Besides," glancing at the doorway where Rose now stood, her father having entered and taken up position next to his wife, "I believe you have some catching up to do."

"Mother," Rose spoke quietly.

"Rose," her mother responded. Although Rose had always called her father, Daddy or Dad, her mother had always been Mother. Mom or Mommy wasn't acceptable. Her mother wasn't strict. More traditional, wanting to follow the examples of previous generations.

"Mother," Rose repeated, taking slow steps toward the woman lying propped in a bed mere paces away, her hands outstretched. Taking hold of her mother's hands, the young woman felt like a child again, one searching for answers, wanting to understand why her parents never came home. "You left me. I thought you were dead." She couldn't stop the trickle of tears once again running down her cheek unchecked. She hadn't cried this much since that day, so long ago, when her aunt tried to explain to her that her parents were lost at sea. Never to return. Dead. She didn't understand death then. She certainly didn't understand it any better as an adult.

"We wanted to reach out to you," her mother sobbed quietly with her daughter. Neither heard the men leave the room, not exactly on tiptoes, but quietly enough for men. "But we couldn't."

"That's what I don't understand." Rose gripped her mother's hands tighter. "Everyone marooned here has to stay. What happened to free will? And the right to choose?"

"It's not so simple," the older woman replied, her voice soft and subtle. It was then Rose realized that her mother didn't look much older than thirty. Rose's age. Also the age Mother had been when she disappeared. How could that be? And yet the king also looked about thirty and he had disappeared about a hundred years ago. Things just didn't add up.

Mother returned the warmth of Rose's firm grasp and gave the younger woman a warm smile. "There is a lot for you to learn and understand, my daughter," she said, stifling a yawn between sniffles. "And you will. I understand you are to meet with the Atlanteans. Soon you will understand. We are the future of humanity." She yawned, wider this time.

"You're tired," Rose patted her mother's hands before releasing them. "You've had a busy night. We'll talk later." She stood up to leave.

"Rose," her mother stopped the younger woman from making a hasty exit. "I am glad you're here."

Rose nodded and left the room, closing the door behind her. When she walked out of the cottage, she realized she hadn't even glanced at the cradle that held her baby brother. Did she want to? It was all too bizarre to take in. She wasn't at all comfortable with this 'chosen' business. She didn't like the idea that she, and others, had been chosen to lead the human race into the future.

Chapter Fifteen

Dr. Burns was waiting for her, sitting on one of the garden chairs at the far end of the yard. Rose's father was nowhere to be seen.

"He had an appointment with the king," the doctor explained, having noticed the young woman's eyes darting around the space, searching. "He said he'd catch up with you later."

She nodded. She understood. All too well. Even as young as she'd been when she last saw them, she had already become accustomed to their flair for self-important duties elsewhere. There was always something or someone more important and she was shoved aside.

The doctor stood up and motioned back the way they had come. "Shall we? The Atlanteans are anxious to meet you."

Rose didn't respond; she merely followed. What else could she do? Nothing was in her control. Only her music made sense, and right now she was being kept away from the piano, the only place she knew that would provide her some sense of solace.

As they approached the castle gardens, Dr. Burns veered off to the left and into a dense thicket of trees. He pushed aside the branches, holding them back so they wouldn't swat Rose in the face while she squeezed through. The path ended abruptly at a stone wall, part of the castle's outer ramifications. A thick, pine door, braced with black metal holsters, was recessed slightly into the stone wall. It was like something out of Tolkien's stories.

As if sensing her thoughts, the doctor chuckled softly and said, "J.R. is here as well. You'll meet him later." A quick glance at the girl's stunned face, he added clarification, "John Ronald Reuel Tolkien," he explained. "Author of "The Lord of the Rings" and many other great works."

"Tolkien's here?" Rose exclaimed.

"Uh-huh," the doctor grunted in response. "He designed the door. Had it built to hobbit specifications."

"Really." Rose gave a noncommittal response as the doctor cranked the large handle and pulled the door open. It creaked, as if it was supposed to creak, giving credence to the idea of entering the home of one of Tolkien's hobbits. There was nothing to see beyond the door. It was like a black hole. Dark. Caverness. As Dr. Burns stepped across the threshold, a light flashed on inside. Rose followed tentatively, jumping when the door behind her slammed shut, with none of the creaking ceremony of its opening.

She found herself standing in a tight space, just enough room for two people: herself and the doctor. Walls surrounded them and the door through which they had walked mere moments before vanished.

"What the…?" She didn't get to finish the explicative, one she was using more frequently since waking up on this mysterious island. She felt a whoosh of air, as if she were falling and being sucked through a descending tunnel at a great speed. She clamped her eyes shut and bit back a scream. When the world around her settled, she slowly opened her eyes to find herself in a large room. Excessively large. One that stretched beyond the scope of her vision. She was alone. Dr. Burns was nowhere to be seen.

She took a step forward, then another. Taking a deep breath and exhaling slowly, she continued her progress. She wasn't sure where she was or where she was going, but a light always shone mere steps ahead of her, like a stage light that focussed on her as the star performer. The light was leading the way.

She reached another door, actually a pair of doors, but before she could raise a hand to knock or to turn a knob, it opened of its own accord, two doors flashing backwards like pages in a book, in the hopes of unraveling a mystery from within. She stepped across the threshold into a brightly lit room. A long table stretched its length and the walls were lined with monitors, not so different from wide screen TVs. Horrific images flashed across each monitor: raging fires, monumental tsunamis, people clustering rooftops of what might have once been a skyrise, their horror evident in the waving hands and expressions of pure panic.

Her eyes surveyed the room panoramically before coming to rest at the far end where a cluster of people were conversing. Or, at least they had been until she entered. Seeing her presence, they quietly left the hive and took seats along the table's length. Dr. Burns was there, as was the king and Rose's father. She also recognized Amadeus, but the others were unfamiliar. Everyone nodded at her, some motioning her into the room.

One man stood taller than the rest, at least seven feet in height. He was lean, his face dark skinned and angular, as if the skin barely stretched across his cheekbones. An equally tall woman, also dark skinned, stood next to him.

"Please, Rosalind Melodious Bell, come in," the man spoke, his voice a deep baritone that echoed across the lengthy expanse of the table. "Take a seat." He motioned to the end, the one remaining empty seat, close to where Rose continued to stand.

"You must have many questions, Rosalind," the woman added her voice, a velvety tone that soothed the soul. "We hope to answer them. But first, allow me to make introductions. I am Helen, a name I took when we first arrived on this planet. I have long since used this name, one which your historians attributed as Queen Helen of Sparta. And this," she pointed to the tall man, "is my father, Zeus. Of equal classical historical fame. We are Atlanteans, from a far-away planet. Zeus, myself and about a dozen others are the last remaining Atlanteans, that we know of, who chose Earth as home. All those years ago. I think the others have provided you with a brief background of our home planet, Atlantea. Our people killed our planet. Destroyed it through greed, war, and disregard for the environment. Much the same as what has happened on Earth. We had hoped to make Earth our home and protect it from the doom that destroyed Atlantea. We tried. We really did. And we failed. At least here we have managed to create a refugee of sorts, to protect the human race. Or at least a select few." Helen paused, allowing her words to sink in.

"The chosen," Rose muttered. She thought her voice was subdued, barely audible. Helen heard. As did the others. She allowed her eyes to seek across the large expanse of the table to capture those of the Atlantean spokesperson. "You made choices. While we live, others die." She waved dramatically at one screen in particular, a view of a rooftop crammed with people waving frantically and presumably calling out for help as a tsunami wave, taller than the building, rushed toward them. Flames etched their way from below. Rose watched in horror as the building crumbled. From the flames? From the impact of the huge wave? She didn't know, but both building and people crumbled to oblivion. "These people are dying, horrific deaths while we sit here, the chosen, deciding a future course. What kind of humanity turns a blind eye to the horrors around them?"

"There was nothing we could do for those people," Helen responded, a note of harshness in her voice. "We couldn't save everyone."

The others sat silently, quietly observing the interchange. Rose's father displayed discomfort at his daughter's outburst, but he didn't speak up. He glanced at Rose briefly before returning his focus, as had the others, to the head of the table. To Helen. And Zeus, who had taken his seat, pondering the outburst quietly.

"No. You couldn't. You made choices," Rose spat back. "You made us the chosen people. You didn't even bother to ask us if we wanted to be chosen. You can't even explain our purpose as the chosen." Her eyes darted from one face at the table to the next before once again resting on Helen. "What is our purpose? To live forever and destroy until we're ignorant and self-centered enough to destroy another planet?"

"You have some pretty strong opinions for a person with so few answers." The male voice boomed across the room. Zeus had spoken. "Perhaps it would be advisable to learn the facts, the answers you so desperately want for all the questions you keep asking others, before coming to such a rash conclusion."

Rose acquiesced, crossed her arms and averted her eyes from Helen to Zeus. "Okay. Let's here the facts. I want some answers. And I want them now."

"Then sit and listen quietly," Zeus commanded. Rose sat abruptly, the voice allowing her no other option, but she held her glare. "Listen to everything we have to say before coming to a conclusion. Before passing judgement." He paused for affect, then spoke again, "For in passing judgement on another, you condemn yourself, because you, the judge, practice the very same things."

"Romans," Rose spoke without expression. "So, you can quote from the Bible."

"Who do you think wrote the Bible?" Zeus countered.

"And now you really believe you are God?" The young woman raised an eyebrow in challenge. "Just as the Greeks once worshipped Zeus, the god of thunder and the sky. Now, you want us all to believe you are the one God?"

"No!" Zeus bellowed, his patience wearing thin. His voice continued with a forced intonation of a storm brewing from within. "Over the centuries, humans searched something to believe in, something to give them faith. I did not insist or even suggest that I was their god or a god of anything. Zeus has been my name since birth, since Atlantea. The Greeks made Zeus into a god. Not me."

Helen interjected, placing a hand on Zeus arm. "We're getting off topic here. We need to explain ourselves. To answer Rose's questions." Her motions and the tone of her voice appeared to have a calming effect on the male Atlantean. He nodded, motioned with his hand for her to continue, and shuffled restlessly in his seat.

The woman, still standing, paced the far end of the room. She waved a hand and a new image appeared on the wall behind her, along with sound effects. A fiery inferno dominated the space, fires raging in such a manner that they appeared to reach beyond the flat, two-dimensional space. This image came with sound effects. It was deafening. Screaming, thunderous crackling, and every obnoxiously indescribable sound possible. Everyone in the room covered their ears to muffle the noise. Helen waved her hand and the sound dissipated, but not completely. She was controlling the presentation and she was allowing a certain amount of noise as a backdrop.

Rose and the others let their hands drop from covering the ears. A few of the congregants ran a weary hand across their foreheads, as if wiping away a pain that wouldn't go away. Helen waited for everyone to settle again, to focus, to pay attention to her and only her.

"This," she said nonchalantly as she dramatically waved a hand at the wall behind her. "This is Atlantea. As we last saw it. More than a millennium ago in your time, a mere century in ours." She snapped her fingers. "This is what our drones picked up on Planet Earth over the past year before the tsunamis destroyed the rest." Her hand waved around the image of another fiery inferno, raging just as much out of control and with similar deafening sound effects as the first image. "Northern British Columbia." She snapped her fingers. Another image. "Northern Ontario and Quebec." Again, she snapped. "California." Snap. "Spain." Snap. "Germany." Snap. "Australia." The worst image yet flashed before them. "The Amazon rainforest. The world's most important ecosystem." She allowed this image to remain on display a little longer, then snapped her fingers again. A satellite image of the earth flashed before them. "Then came the rash impact of multiple earthquakes around the world: Tibet, California, Haiti, Siberia. And the phenomenal forces of nature swirling up the oceans, causing hurricanes and cyclones of monumental intensity. And, the final blow, the Yellowstone volcano that started a chain reaction of volcanic activity in Hawaii, Costa Rica, Italy, Iceland, Siberia, Japan. Volcanoes, earthquakes, monumental storm systems and, the final blow, the tsunami that washed across the remains."

Her arms raised and her hands pointed to images flashing around the room. "This is what's left of your planet, Rose. This destruction. It's not all a result of careless management of the ecosystems. It's not all an Armageddon that began with pointless conflicts and wars. It's not all due to the tons of plastics dumped in the waters globally. But humanity's abuse of their planet contributed to the final catastrophic event – its annihilation."

She stopped. Allowed her words and the images to tell the rest of the story. Rose broke the silence. "And yet here we are," she waved her own arms, indicating those seated at the table. "All of us and more out there," she waved behind her, indicating the only way she knew to enter this space. "Here we are, alive and well and prospering. In the middle of what was once the Caribbean. While the rest of the planet destroys itself and people in the billions suffer horrific deaths, we prosper. Why? Because we were chosen. And how is it that this place can buffer the forces from beyond and protect a specific geographic place from total destruction? From Armageddon?" She paused briefly to catch her breath, but she wasn't done. Not by a longshot. "And, should we continue to survive, what next? Do we re-inhabit the earth? What's left of it? Do we start over as Noah did after the flood? And, if we do, what's to say this won't happen all over again? We can't stop the wheels of destructive behavior. Not forever. Perhaps not at all."

As she finished her last words, a red light began flashing and a siren pierced the relative calm that had settled in as she spoke. Words came across from some sort of loudspeaker, "Conflict in Section B. Secure the area. Conflict in Section B."

Rose raised her hands in supplication. "I rest my case. Even here, even in this so-called paradise, there is conflict."

Helen stood up straighter, pushing her shoulders back and leveling her eyes on Rose's. "The dispute is being taken care of. It's at the refugee camp at the far end of the island. Nothing to concern us."

"Nothing to concern us?" Rose retaliated. "Refugee camp?"

Waving her hand at the images depicting crowded rooftops of people waving and reaching out for help, Helen continued, "You were quick to judge, demanding why we didn't help these survivors. But we did help them. As many as we could."

"And dumped them in refugee camps." Rose shook her head in disgust. "Why am I so different? Why are all the people here and the other great minds you've rescued over the years different?"

"Everyone is processed," Helen snapped back. "Even you."

"Processed?" The young woman wasn't stepping down. She didn't like what she was hearing. She didn't care for this sense of privileged selection. "And then what? Some are allowed to stay? Infiltrated into our tiny little community? Others discarded? Or, worse, made into slaves?"

"We have no slaves here." Zeus slammed the palms of his hands on the table and stood up. "Enough of this. If you don't like it here, you're welcome to go back to where you came from."

"To what?" Rose challenged. "There's nothing left!"

"Exactly!" Zeus retorted. "So, either we choose to get along and work together, or we disband and make our own way in a world that really, for all intents and purposes, no longer exists."

"And if it no longer exists," Rose countered. "What are we supposed to do here? Now? What is this place? And how is it that this island, this community, has survived the total destruction of Earth?"

"Good questions." Helen was regaining a sense of calm. "Perhaps we could all agree to discuss something useful, instead of pitting words against one another. Rose wants to understand this place." She placed a hand on Zeus's arm. The calming effect was obvious. He nodded and sat back down.

"Then let's talk," he said. He waited for the others to settle. Those who hadn't contributed to the heated exchange had shuffled restlessly in their seats. With Zeus, Helen and Rose no longer combatting with words, everyone breathed a sigh of relief. "Dulces Sueños Island is actually our spaceship, Rose. Or, I should clarify, what is left of our spaceship." He paused briefly to allow the words to sink in. Noticing the widening of the young woman's eyes, he realized he had her undivided attention. He continued, "Our spaceship was designed to endure all kinds of atmospheric and destructive anomalies. It was also designed to blend into the surrounding environment. When we first discovered Earth, we settled just off the coast of Egypt and lived amongst the early peoples you've probably read about in the Bible. We tried to influence people inhabiting this general geographic area in a positive way, the Israelites and the Egyptians. Some listened, like Moses. But most did not, like the pharaohs of Egypt who only sought greater glory in this world and the next. We helped them design and build the pyramids, hoping they would learn from us. Instead, their greed took root and they sought domination, not just of the Israelites, but domination of Atlanteans as well. Sadly, we lost some good people during that era."

"I thought you couldn't die," Rose interrupted. "Your nanorobots saved me multiple times and I'm sure they've saved others. Why not your people?"

"Some injuries are too severe," Zeus answered in a somber tone. "And our nanorobots were still in the development stage. We hadn't fully perfected their abilities."

"But you have now," the young woman challenged.

"To some extent," Zeus conceded. "We hadn't taken into consideration possible allergic reactions to the materials used in their construction. That is, until you had an almost deadly reaction. That has been modified. Hopefully there won't be many, if any, further complications. It's taken us centuries to perfect nanotechnology."

"And it's still not perfect," Helen interceded. "Nothing is. Back to the story. When it became evident that we couldn't help the Egyptians see a better way, we had to leave. The Israelites had already followed Moses to the Promised Land. We had learned from them as they learned from us. We learned their stories of creation, or Adam and Eve, of Noah and his ark, his attempt to save humanity."

"Another failed attempt," Rose noted. "And you believe you can do better?"

"We keep hoping and trying," Helen admitted. "There never is a perfect solution. We tried with the Romans and the Greeks. The Greeks listened for awhile. They called our ship, which we blended into the landscape as a grand city, Atlantis. When we gave up on them and decided to move on, they made stories of the mythical city of Atlantis and how it disappeared. We settled in the center of the ocean. Here. Only venturing out on occasion to try and make a difference. We tried with the great rulers of England, France and Russia. No one would bend their way for the sake of all of humanity. Greed. It's too powerful a human trait."

"And then people started disappearing mysteriously in this area that became known as the Bermuda Triangle." Rose studied the faces of everyone seated at the table, some who should be several hundred years old. "And you created an Utopia where everyone lives forever."

"Perhaps not forever, Rose," Helen pointed out. "But, having studied your Bible stories, I'm sure you have noticed that some people do live into their hundreds."

"Scientists suggested it was merely a different means of measuring the years," Rose argued.

"Perhaps in some ways they're right," Zeus suggested. "What is time, after all? Isn't it all relative?"

"You're starting to sound like Einstein," the young woman chuckled softly, shaking her head in disbelief.

"He should be here," Zeus noted, a semblance of a smile barely showing. "But he probably got wrapped up in his latest mathematical calculations." Glancing around the room, he asked, "Has anyone seen Albert this morning?"

"How could Einstein be here when the greatest scientist of all time donated his brain for scientific research?"

"A good question," the doctor broke the silence of the gathered humans. "I was there when Albert supposedly took his last breath. He was the one who suggested I remove his brain once he was truly dead. The opportunity never arose. We, Albert and I, colleagues from way back, were spirited away by these people. Albert's body was replaced by a look-alike. The brain researchers have studied for decades, really wasn't the brain of the greatest mathematical genius of all time."

"So, the people chosen and collected for this commune were not always lost at sea in the Caribbean?" Rose queried. "This is becoming more complicated all the time."

Another shrill siren broke through the confines of the room. The lights flickered and the wall screens snapped off. A collective gasp penetrated the air.

"This meeting is adjourned," Zeus spoke with authority, standing up abruptly and turning to make a hasty exit.

Helen glanced around the room nervously. "My apologies. This meeting will have to continue at another time. It would appear there's been a breach in our protective devices. Perhaps the infraction at the refugee compound caused this breach." Her eyes rested on Rose's. "I am sorry. But this must be taken care of immediately. Feel free to ask the others questions. They will answer as best they can." Looking again at the others, she instructed. "Now, go." As quickly as she spoke, she was gone, rushing in Zeus's wake.

A voice announced dryly over the intercom. "This is a lockdown situation. Please make haste to the nearest building and seal all openings. This is not a drill. I repeat. This is not a drill."

"What the…?" Rose didn't have the opportunity to finish her question. The clangs and bangs sealed her inside the room with the others. Like a vacuum sucking out all the fresh air, she felt a tightening in her chest. She moved over toward her father, seeking comfort in his presence as a child would with a parent. As she sat down next to him, he gripped her hand. "Will Mother be all right?" she whispered in a strained tone. "And my baby brother?"

"I hope so, Rose," he replied solemnly. "I hope so." The lights dimmed. The steady drone of the vents pumping air into the room went silent. And the lights went out.

Chapter Sixteen

There was a collective gasp, but no one spoke. Everyone remained where they were. There was no sense in trying to get up and move around. It was pitch black and, with the doors sealed shut, they had nowhere to go. Finally, a purr of an engine kicked in and a flush of fresh air filled the space. Rose let out a breath of relief, noticing the collective sound as the others did, too. A glimmer of light sprinkled into action, dim, but sufficient to see around the room.

"The emergency generators have kicked in," Rose's father spoke quietly. "The Atlanteans balked at the concept, insisting their systems would never fail."

"But they just did," Rose pointed out.

"For the first time in thousands of years," Dr. Burns noted. "I'm glad you insisted, James," he spoke to Rose's father. "We would soon be suffocating without the failsafe backup generators."

"Hopefully they'll hold until the real problem is diagnosed," James responded. Turning to his daughter, he clasped her hand more firmly in his own, the warmth seeping up her arms with reassurance. "You asked some pretty difficult questions, Rose. You challenged Helen and Zeus as no one has challenged them before. At least, not in my time here."

"Nor mine either," Fred, the king, added his voice, the first time he had spoken since Rose had entered the room. "And I've been here longer than your father. We've all had our questions and concerns, much like yours. But we were so wrapped up in working toward the common good of creating Novae Terrae."

"It isn't right," Rose launched into her concerns. "It's just too good to be true. To be real. It's too much like Aldous Huxley's *Brave New World*."

"Without the test tube babies," James interjected. "My son was not conceived in a test tube."

"Wasn't he?" Rose shifted so she could study her father more intently. He hadn't aged. He should look at least twenty-five or thirty years older than her, but he had the skin and hair color of someone her own age. "How can you be so sure?"

"Well I…" he stuttered in response, nervous at the idea of explaining the details to his daughter, even though she was old enough to know the facts of life.

He didn't get to complete his answer. Dr. Burns took over. "I have monitored your mother's pregnancy right from the beginning," he spoke with assurance. "And, if there were a lab somewhere creating test tube babies, I'm sure I would know about it."

"Would you?" She shifted her glance to the doctor's. He didn't meet her eye-to-eye. None of the others would either. "What else aren't you telling me? What else is there about this place that isn't right and no one will address?" Her eyes darted from one person to the next before coming to a rest on her father. Even he wouldn't meet her glance, sitting with head bent studying their clasped hands. "Tell me!" she insisted.

"Rose," her father took up the challenge, answering in a slow calm voice. "It's not perfect. Nothing is. But it's all that's left. Earth has been destroyed. It's toxic out there. Very little dry land, if any. Our home is gone. Forever."

"So they tell you," Rose wasn't convinced. "How do we know they're not manipulating our perception of events outside the Bermuda Triangle? How do we know what they're saying is true?"

"Facts speak for themselves," Fred answered. "Earth has been doomed for some time and humanity was helping progress the end of our planet. It was bound to happen sooner or later."

"But how do we know for a fact that it's happened?" She wasn't giving up. She had to know. For sure. She needed reassurance. She needed confirmation.

The room was silent. Hands shuffled imaginary papers on the table and eyes were rivetted on their movement. Finally, Fred broke the unsettling void, his voice echoing through the seemingly soundless space. "I was out there when the first wave struck. The first tsunami." His voice was serene, calm, almost a whisper. "It was horrific. It is real, Rose. Very real."

Shock registered on Rose's face. "How were you 'out there'?" she asked, using her fingers to air quote the last two words. "I thought residents of this commune didn't go and come back. You either stayed, or left permanently like your wife did."

The king bristled noticeably at the mention of his wife. "That was a long time ago, Rose," he responded, an edge catching in his tone of voice. "I prefer not to think of that time, to think of her." His fingers lightly drummed the table's surface. "However, you're right, Rose. We don't normally leave and come back. Lately, things have been precarious even here and multiple manned drones have been sent out to monitor the situation beyond our protective sphere. I was on one of those manned drones. Your father," he nodded at James, "was on another and Dr. Burns was manning yet another. There were at least a dozen drones sent out in all directions. Mostly manned, but some were not. We sent back data of what we witnessed; rescued people as we could and when we could. The last refugees, as you describe them, were rescued from the top of the Burj Khalifa in Dubai, the world's tallest building and the only one we could find that wasn't totally submerged. You saw the image on the screen when you entered this room. Fires were climbing up the remaining feet to the rooftop and massive waves continued to crash against the structure. We rescued about a hundred people and would have saved more if the building hadn't crumbled from the impact of the final wave and the weakened structure desecrated by the fires."

The young woman settled back in her chair, released her hold on James's hand. "So, those were the only ones you saved? In the entire world?" It was more question than statement.

"The last time we were out, yes," Fred answered. "We saved others at the beginning of the massive destruction. From different tall structures around the world. But it wasn't enough. We weren't fast enough. The powers of destruction were faster. We tried, Rose. We did try. And we witnessed first hand the end of Earth as we knew it."

"How do you know for sure there aren't any more out there waiting to be rescued?" she waved her hands dramatically. "Have you covered every inch of this planet?"

"No, Rose," James replied in a monotone voice. "We haven't checked everywhere. Drones continue to go out daily, seeking, searching, hoping. We even scan the depths of the flooded planet in the hopes of finding some submarines with live human beings on board. But so far, nothing more."

"But how could these drones survive the forces that destroyed the rest of the world?" She wasn't giving up. There was still something nagging at the back of her mind. Something wasn't right. "And what about Air Force One? Didn't it manage to escape? And other big nations must have had their escape plans ready to put into action. What happened to all the world leaders?"

Suddenly the lights were on full strength and the click of the doors unlocking shattered the silence that followed Rose's final questions. The gathering rose in unison and made their way to the exit. Single file, they walked out into the sunshine and made haste in different directions, presumably to assess any potential damage to their private domains.

Rose's father gave a quick wave and rushed off in the direction of his cabin, with barely a, "See you later," comment. Dr. Burns and the king were making their way in the general direction of the castle. Exhausted from the morning's activities, Rose decided to follow. Where else would she go? she reasoned.

The two men motioned her forward and soon she was walking with one on either side of her. They walked in silence for a few minutes, allowing the sounds of nature to sooth their nerves, which were still unsettled from the lockdown.

"Is everyone locked into whatever building they are in at the time of a crisis?" Rose broke the silence.

"Yes," Fred answered. "It's the Atlanteans way of protecting the innocent while dealing with a problem. There haven't been many over the centuries, but quite a few recently."

"Why?" She was insistent with her questioning. She wanted answers. She needed to understand.

"Rose," Dr. Burns spoke in his usual calm voice. "Sometimes it's better to observe and learn than to ask too many questions."

"Safer, too," Fred muttered under his breath, his feet shuffling along as they marched up the slight incline leading to the castle.

"Why safer?" She couldn't stop her questions. Why should she?

"People rescued here have not always been allowed to stay," the doctor answered simply. "Too many questions. Too many challenges against Atlantean authority. It's too risky to be so demanding. Live and learn. It's not so bad."

The king continued to walk along slowly, eyes focussed on the ground he tread upon. Finally, he spoke. "My wife was one of those who asked too many questions." He didn't say any more, merely picking up his pace and moving ahead of the other two.

When Fred was far enough ahead, Dr. Burns spoke softly, loud enough for only Rose to hear. "It was difficult when his wife disappeared. He was quite torn with wanting to follow her and wanting to stay and lead this brave new world that the Atlanteans were trying to build. Fred was sold on the idea of a fair, equal opportunity, loving community. His wife was not. She questioned everything. Challenged everything. Life is a challenge no matter where you are, Rose. Sometimes it's best to accept, watch and learn. Your questions will be answered, but not instantaneously and certainly not all at once. And challenging those who really did save your life, is not such a good idea."

"Where would they send me, then, if they decided to get rid of me?" Rose muttered another question. "There's nothing out there. Or so everyone claims."

"Exactly," the doctor responded. "You wouldn't survive a few minutes out there; the air is so toxic. There is no dry land and the waters are rough and unpredictable at best. You are better off here, so you'd be well advised to accept things and…"

"To watch and learn."

"Exactly."

Chapter Seventeen

Upon returning to the castle, Rose parted company with the two men and went to her room to freshen up. She walked slowly around the room, glancing at the growing treasures, rescued from her home. She touched them, felt their warmth, recalled the significance of each item. They had planned this. The Atlanteans had an agenda. They had decided long before the storm that hit the cruise ship that Rose would be brought to Dulces Sueños Island. How many others had been manipulated into believing they had been rescued? Everyone here, except the more recently arrived refugees, had been chosen. But why? Would she ever know? Was it worth the time, the effort, the stress of constantly asking questions? Especially now that she knew there was a danger lurking behind each question she asked.

She walked a full circle around the room, ending at the door. Reaching for the handle, she allowed her eyes to circle the room again. With a deep sigh, she pulled open the door and made her way down to the conservatory. There was only one recourse that would sooth her troubled soul: music. She was relieved to encounter no one as she traipsed the now familiar route. All was quiet. Too quiet. Just as it had been first thing this morning. Her piano sat majestically in the center of the conservatory, beckoning her to come and play. All sense of unease dwindled and vanished as she sat down and allowed her fingers to move across the keyboard.

She wasn't sure how long she had been playing. Time was an anomaly when she immersed herself in music. She had played through most of her repertoire: Mozart, of course, and Beethoven, a few of the other classics like Bach and Haydn, before launching into the Romantics: Chopin and Schumann (both Robert and

Clara). Finally, she had worked her way through the twentieth century compositions of Debussy, Torjussen, Schafer, Louie and many others.

Finally, she stopped. She could take no more. Her fingers ached. Her back and shoulders throbbed. She was tired. Silence engulfed the conservatory, where once tinkling notes permeated the space. As the vibrations settled and the air stilled, the young woman breathed in, slowly, deeply. She was refreshed. She hadn't lost her concerns, but her music had been the balm she needed.

She was startled out of her reverie by the sound of hands clapping. She had an audience. Not a large one, as the clapping only sounded like one set of hands. She glanced toward the sound and smiled when she noticed Amadeus approaching the piano.

"You play like an angel," he said. "Mind you, I can't say I understand most of what you just performed, but it is interesting, to say the least. I am delighted they took my recommendation to bring you to our Dulces Sueños Island."

"Your recommendation?" Rose's eyebrows lifted to accentuate her surprise.

"Yes, my dear," the maestro spoke softly. "We all have the opportunity to make choices. Or, I should say, we did. Now there is no one left to choose. And we must move forward with those we have adopted. You will see, my dear. No one has all the answers. But life here is good and the plan, as I understand it, is to start a new world outside of this isolated area. To begin again."

"Like after Noah's flood," the young woman queried.

"Exactly. Hopefully this time we'll get it right." He rubbed his hands together, an air of excitement evident. "Now. It is time to meet the arts community of Dulces Sueños Island. There are many who are anxious to meet you. Claude, Wolfgang, Johanne and some others whose music I do not understand. Come." He held out a hand. "I shall take you to the Conservatoire de Musique de Dulces Sueños Island."

"A real conservatory?" Rose exclaimed, standing up and following Amadeus's lead. "Here on Dulces Sueños Island?"

"A real conservatory," Amadeus responded with a note of pride in his voice. "We have all levels of learning, all subjects available. This is a very advanced community. Your parents lead the natural sciences department at the university." The maestro chatted amiably as the two exited the castle by the conservatory doors.

Rose breathed in deeply. Fresh air had been difficult to enjoy before she arrived at this island. Perhaps she never really had experienced breathing in truly fresh air. The planet had been so badly polluted, damaged from centuries of misuse and abuse. Armageddon was not unexpected. Every doomsday prediction suggested a cataclysmic demise at any moment in time.

Looking around her, she realized that it must be mid-afternoon. Where had the day gone? The early morning impromptu performance, followed by meeting her parents and newborn brother. Then the meeting with the Atlanteans which really hadn't resolved any of her unanswered questions. How long had she been plundering her way through the musical repertoire of the centuries? It must have been several hours.

Realizing Amadeus was the last one to speak, the young woman shook her head to clear the cobwebs and tried to focus on his last comment. "My parents?" she half-asked.

"Yes," Amadeus repeated, not fully cognisant that his previous comment had gone relatively unheard. "They head the Department of Natural Sciences at the University of Dulces Sueños Island."

"My parents?" She glanced at the maestro. He nodded. "Heading the Natural Sciences Department?" He nodded again. "And there's a university here?" Another nod.

"Come along, my dear." He picked up his pace, the trimming on his crimson pelisse with the shiny gold embroidery and the matching gold-laced bicorn hat reflected in the bright sun and sent sparks of light in every direction. He marched as if he were going on stage to perform: tall, proud, determined and confident. He looked every bit the dandy composer and performer that he had been in the eighteenth century. Even his knee-high, black leather boots, complete with the bright shiny buckle at the ankle, glistened with perfection. "You will see it all."

It wasn't a long walk. In fact, amazingly, everything on the island appeared to be within walking distance. Rose hadn't noted that observation earlier, but it was just one more thing to add to the list of troubling coincidentals. She felt a prickling sensation rattling up and down her spine. It was as if someone was following them. Following her. Spying on her. Were her thoughts also being monitored? These nanorobots swirling through her blood vessels might be recording everything about her, from how many breaths she took each minute to how many questions she asked in her mind.

Blinking her eyes, she tried to erase the troubling thoughts plaguing her. She picked up her pace, keeping time with the maestro's steady footsteps. They left the castle grounds behind them, walked down into a valley of lush green vegetation, dotted with barns, farmhouses and livestock. The path, wide enough for two people to walk side by side, was well worn, but definitely not something a motorized vehicle could navigate.

"Are there no cars on this island?" she blurted out before she could stop herself. "No trucks?"

Amadeus shook his head and picked up his pace another notch. "No need. We can navigate this island very well on foot or on horseback if necessary. Cars and trucks pollute."

"So do people and animals," Rose muttered under her breath.

Amadeus didn't respond. He carried on as if he hadn't heard what she said.

They mounted a slight hill and Rose gasped at the sight that lay before her. "Wow!" was all she could think to say.

Amadeus waved his hand dramatically as if conducting a symphony orchestra. "And there it is. Conservatoire de Musique de Dulces Sueños Island. And over to the right, nestled between those tall hills, is the rest of the University of Dulces Sueños Island."

"Impressive."

"The Atlanteans favor education over everything else," Amadeus explained. "Without education, we cannot progress."

"And without music," Rose added, "life would be a mistake." Turning to the maestro, she asked, "Will I be meeting your friend, Friedrich Nietzsche?"

"Friedrich and so many others," Amadeus answered bluntly. "Come along. The great halls of music and the arts await."

"And the arts?" Rose queried, having to quicken her pace, again, to keep up.

"Yes," the maestro, for his several hundred years of living, didn't appear the least bit out of breath from the brisk pace he was setting. "Didn't I explain?" Noticing Rose's blank expression, he continued with a huff that bordered on frustration. "You must pay attention, young lady," he gently scolded. "The Conservatoire is the center for all the arts on Dulces Sueños Island, music being its most prominent art." He puffed his chest out with a certain amount of pride. "Of course, Rembrandt might argue otherwise.

"Rembrandt?" Rose exclaimed. "He's here, too? Will I meet him?"

"Yes, my dear. You will meet everyone." The pace quickened again and Rose had to jog to keep up.

As they reached what appeared to be the entrance to the Conservatoire, Rose took in the building itself and the multiple structures that lined the path on which they trod. The Conservatoire was vast, with many domes and turrets. It almost put the castle to shame with its stark white brick that all but glistened in the afternoon sun. The buildings they passed were impressive, too, some with bell tower entrances, others with gold covered domes encompassing the entire roof.

She let out a gasp and stopped abruptly. "Amadeus. These are churches. And mosques and synagogues. People have places to worship here?"

"Of course," Amadeus did a sharp about-turn and came face-to-face with his companion. "Religion is a vital part of humanity. For good or bad, it is our history and the means by which we humans understand and appreciate the world around us."

"But," the young woman stammered, waving her hands around the enclave of religious buildings. "All in the same area? All neighbors, so to speak? Do they all get along? And how do they fit in with the arts?"

"The leaders of each religious group have an agreement with the Atlanteans," came the answer with great gravity. "Put simply, they have all agreed to disagree, but only verbally. There is no violence or bloodshed on Dulces Sueños Island. It is forbidden. Any physical violence results in instant banishment. And, considering what's out there, which is nothing, banishment would mean certain death. As for associating with the arts, perhaps my dear friend, Michelangelo will clarify the connection better than I. Now," the maestro's voice barely masked his growing impatience. "Let's go meet the others. Time's a-wasting."

Rose chuckled and had to jog, again, to keep pace, for Amadeus was almost jogging himself, his long cloak billowing in a glowing wave behind him. "My aunt used that phrase. Frequently."

"It's one I picked up from your mother," Amadeus confessed as the two walked through a grand archway into a small courtyard enclosure.

Rose wanted to pause and study what she saw. It was breathtaking. Michelangelo's famous sculpture "David" and Rodin's "The Thinker" were nothing compared to the grand sculptures in stone and bronze that graced the courtyard, dominating every available space.

"Michelangelo. Here. And Leonardo? And Rodin?" There was no answer. She didn't need one.

Amadeus led her through the maze of sculptures, up a grand set of stone steps and into the building. Rose paused briefly at the threshold to allow her eyes to adjust after being in the bright sun. When she was able to focus again, she marveled at the mosaic tiled floor that suggested the master artisans of the Byzantine era and the busts that sat on pedestals around the entrance hall reminded her of Greek and Roman busts. The maestro was right: the Conservatoire housed all the arts.

Strains of music filtered down the hall, accompanied by muffled voices, some excited, others heated in argumentative discussions. Rose breathed deeply. She already felt at home.

Chapter Eighteen

Quite simply, it was amazing. Rose had performed the works of masters from across the centuries, but now, she was meeting so many of them. She followed Amadeus down a long hall toward the steady drum of voices, entering a large room that was packed with people of all ages, sizes, male, female, and transgender. All were dressed in outfits that suggested the era in which they were known to live and work. Some of the outfits were rather flamboyant, like Chopin and Liszt in their formal black tuxedoes with flashy tails, snuggly hugging their torso and sporting the classic white gloves they always wore when performing. Others, like Robert Schumann were dowdy and nonchalant. The artists were another set of creative wardrobes, painters and sculptors dubbed in the medium of their trade: splashings of oil paint or stone dust, depending on whether they were a painter or a sculptor. But, underneath their drapery of necessity and period style, they were all the same: creative minds bent on creating the next great work of art, be it music, painting, sculpture, dance, literature, or even photography and multi-media.

She had been warmly welcomed by all. Beethoven had greeted her with what she would have expected as his usual gruff demeanor. Amadeus whispered in her ear as the temperamental, once deaf musical genius stumbled over. "He's still as grumpy as ever. But at least he has his hearing again. Those things the Atlanteans inserted inside us have done wonders in keeping us young, healthy and fully functioning. You should hear his twenty-first symphony."

"But he only wrote nine," Rose argued. Amadeus didn't answer. He didn't have to.

"I have been here a long time," Beethoven grumbled. "Far too long, if you ask me. But at least I can hear what I compose."

"His work doesn't sound so angry any more," someone off to the side muttered just loud enough for Rose to hear.

She smiled at the famous composer and ducked her head in greeting. "Maestro Beethoven. It is an honor."

"Call me Ludwig and I shall call you Rose. And you shall play my latest composition, a piano concerto which I wrote specifically with you in mind."

Rose blushed. "I'm honored, sir."

"Ludwig," he corrected.

"Ludwig." She favored him with a gracious smile.

And so, the greetings and accolades continued. By the time she had circumnavigated the large hall several times, Rose's head was spinning. So much talent. Saved. Preserved. But for what?

She managed to avoid the actual ritual of shaking hands in greeting, she used the fist pump and her glowing smile, a musician's survival strategy to protect the hands, the instruments of her artistry, from an over-zealous, firm gripping hand-shaker. Even the artists appreciated her respect for the hands of creativity, as did they. Some of the women had actually given her a hug. It had been awkward, as she had never been much of a hugging person. She went along with the flow, accepting and being accepted. If she had to accept this community run by Atlanteans for what it was, a privileged commune of the chosen, then at least she had her music and her contacts in the world of fine art to keep her content.

Later, over dinner at the castle, she shuffled the fork around the plate in front of her, absently reminiscing on the day's events.

"I believe the catch-phrase is, a penny for your thoughts?" the king broke the silence. Young Prince Edouard chuckled. He had been noticeably absent all day, except during Rose's impromptu early morning performance.

Rose glanced up at the only two companions seated with her this evening: the king and the prince. "So much to think about. And, I believe the phrase is dated now. The last I heard, there were no pennies being used in any monetary system in the world." She shrugged at the surprised look on Freddy's face. "Where's everyone else this evening? The doctor? Maria?"

"The good doctor is doing his rounds," Fred explained. "Making sure everyone's all right after the excitement earlier today. Maria usually accompanies him when she's not tied up caring for a patient."

"Like me?" Rose couldn't help but smile.

The king returned her smile with one of his own. "Like you." He dipped his head toward Rose's plate. "Now eat up. You've hardly taken a bite."

"And it's good," Edouard piped up. "There's chocolate cake for dessert, so save some room for that."

They shared a laugh and Rose began the process of eating, more a mechanical motion than a hunger for food. It was tasty, well prepared. In fact, it was one of her favorite dishes: chicken cacciatore with a side of vegetables. It wasn't a multi-course meal complete with appetizers and salads, but rather a simple fare of a main course and dessert. Which, as Edouard promised, was chocolate cake. Another favorite. Just enough. She should be enjoying it. Was her mind playing tricks on her? Or was she seriously too involved in reminiscing the events of the day?

When the final morsel of cake was wiped from her plate, Edouard asked to be excused. "Homework," Fred instructed.

Typically, the boy groaned. "I'm always doing homework. Why do I have to know everything?"

"He's still going to school?" Rose asked. "After a hundred years of being a child, slowly growing up, shouldn't he know what he needs to know by now?"

"Yeah!" Edouard perked up at the defense coming from across the table. He flashed Rose a grateful smile.

The king didn't answer right away. When he did, it was with slow, thoughtful purpose. "Edouard needs to prepare himself to be a ruler. Not just any ruler, but one that will lead the new world, Novae Terrae, for many millennia into the future. There is much to learn: history, languages and the arts, mathematics and science. He must learn as much as he can, so he understands and appreciates the world around him. So, he can make Novae Terrae a better place to live than the world we left behind."

"When does he get to grow up?" Rose asked. "And, in his hundred years of living, was he ever allowed to play? To be a child? To be with children his age?"

"Yes." The king tossed his napkin beside his dessert plate. "Enough questions. Edouard, you know what you have to do."

"Yes, Father," the boy responded, his voice dejected, eyes downcast. He slowly pivoted away from the table and made a slow exit, his feet dragging across the floor.

"Now, Rose." Fred stood. "I have arranged for us to have coffee on the terrace. It's a pleasant evening. There should be a spectacular sunset shortly and, with the clear sky, we'll have a charming display of stars to lighten the sky. Shall we?"

Rose folded and placed her napkin beside her plate. No dramatics, not like the king. She stood up gracefully and glanced at her host, if that's what he was. "I'd prefer some green tea, if that's possible."

The king merely nodded, lifted his arm for her to take and, once she had slipped her arm into his, he led the way toward the French doors that opened onto a large balcony. "I shall see to your request," he motioned Rose to be seated, while he exited briefly to put in the order.

She chose to stand and walked over to the stone railing, leaning lightly on it to allow her some balance as she glanced at the glowing reds, pinks and yellows that wrapped its warmth around the horizon, leaving behind the clear sky Fred had promised. She breathed deeply and sighed with contentment.

The king sidled up beside her, saying, "The tea and coffee will be here shortly." Waving a hand at the display of color, he added, "I did promise you a beautiful sunset, followed by a clear sky."

"Yes, you did." She peaked out of the corner of her eyes, studying the man next to her. He was handsome. For his age of over a hundred years, he didn't look much older than she was. And he wore his fine clothes with the ease of a man used to being well dressed and presentable at all times. "Makes me think you have some psychic powers to predict the weather."

Fred chuckled softly. "No, my dear. Mere observation. I'm not always right, but I like to think that I'm right most of the time." He reached across the space that separated them and took her hand in his. At the precious moment that his hand touched hers, music drifted up from the grounds below. "Ah! Finally! I had feared our chamber group wouldn't show."

"Chamber group?" Rose pulled her hand away, as if sparks had ignited, sending nervous energy up her arm and along her spine. She shivered imperceptibly, whether for the sudden loss of contact, or the contact that preceded, she couldn't be sure.

"Rose." Not to be deterred, Fred reached out and this time took both her hands in his. "I would like us to be friends. In fact, I would like us to be more than just friends. It's been a hundred years since my wife left me. I have been alone for a long time." He pulled the young woman closer. Releasing one hand, he traced a finger down Rose's cheek and leaned in for a kiss. At least, that appeared to be his intent.

Rose gasped and jumped back, pulling her hands free. "Fred. Your Majesty. I don't know. This is quite sudden. We've only just met." Her hands reached her cheeks as she struggled to fight the growing heat that escalated up her neck and across her face. She was saved from saying anything else by the arrival of their beverages.

Fred stepped back as well, nodding his head. "I understand. You need time. But time is not in our favor. The Atlanteans…" He didn't finish.

Rose's eyes bulged. Something was being planned without her knowledge. Something that involved her and had nothing to do with her musical talent. "What about the Atlanteans?" she almost snarled her question, taking a few more steps backwards, away from the king, the man who tried to kiss her. She shook her head and would have stepped further back, but the heel of her shoe caught in one of the stones and she realized, too late, that she had backed to the edge of the top step leading down into the gardens.

She heard Fred's startled exclamation, "Rose. No. Stop," as she tumbled backwards, her back hitting the sharp stone edges as she rolled down. The last thing she remembered before blacking out was an intense flash of pain.

Chapter Nineteen

Rose's eyes fluttered open. She winced. The light was bright. It sent arrows through her eyeballs, deep into the skull. A shadow flickered above, flashing a light back and forth over her face. A voice accompanied the shadow.

"You're going to have to stop the dramatics, my dear." It was Dr. Burns. "The nanorobots can only do so much to repair damages and keep you well."

Recollections of her fall fluttered through her mind as she winced her eyes open wider. "What happened?" She remembered. Sort of. She couldn't believe she had fallen backwards down the stone patio steps.

"You fell," Dr. Burns stated flatly. "Quite dramatically. Backwards. Rolled down several stone steps before coming to a rest at the bottom. You're very lucky nothing was broken."

"How did I get here?" she glanced around, now that her eyes were starting to focus. She was in her room.

"The king carried you," he said grimly, flicking his eyebrows up to accentuate his thoughts. "Again," he added.

"Again?" she asked.

"Well, it was the king who carried you from the beach the day you washed ashore," the doctor elaborated. "What made you back up so carelessly?"

"I..." she stuttered. She tried to shrug her shoulders, but the motion made her wince. "I had a shock," was all she could think to say.

"He tried to propose, didn't he?" Dr. Burns let loose a deep sigh. "I told him it was too soon. I did say it might spook you. And that it did. I am so sorry, Rose. After a hundred years or more, we on Dulces Sueños Island tend to lose track of time. And we are an impatient bunch." He stepped away from the bed as the door opened and a woman entered. Turning, he greeted her, "Keep her quiet, Maria. No visitors. No exertion. Wake her every few hours."

"But her parents are here, Dr. Burns," Maria spoke quietly. "And the king wants to see her."

"No," the doctor exclaimed. "Not now. Perhaps later." Patting Rose's hand gently, he gave her some orders as well. "Rest. The meds I injected earlier and the nanorobots will do their work. You'll feel better later today. For now, just rest."

"I'll stay with her, doctor," Maria reassured him, as the doctor let himself out.

Rose's eyelids felt heavy. She wanted desperately to give into the intense lure of sleep, but she couldn't. Not yet. She had questions. Still. Too many questions.

"Maria," she called the older woman to her bedside. "Please tell me. I need to know. How much of me is still me?" It was an intense question, one that had plagued her since she first found out about the nanorobots. It plagued her more now, after the fall. If she had fallen backwards, down the stone steps to the garden (and there must be at least a dozen steps), she could easily have broken her back or her neck, or cracked open her skull. She felt around her head, seeking proof of injuries. There were none. She had aches and pains stretching from one end of her torso to the other, but nothing more than she would feel after tripping over a twig in the woods. It didn't make sense. Unless, she shuddered at the thought. Unless she wasn't human anymore.

Maria came and sat on the side of the bed, taking Rose's hands in her own. Releasing a deep breath, she spoke calmly. "Rose," she said. "As you are probably starting to surmise, you are no more than a shell of your original human form. Your mind and memory are intact, but your body is pretty much consumed by nanorobots. They protect you." She paused, as if debating how much more to say. "Your fall was rather severe. Had it not been for the nanorobots, you wouldn't be talking to me now."

"And when I was washed ashore?" Rose asked.

"You were on death's door," Maria admitted. "Without the nanorobots, you wouldn't have survived."

"So, basically, I'm a robot." The young woman cringed as she spoke those words.

Maria merely nodded.

"And so are you and all the others," Rose surmised.

Maria nodded again.

"So, basically, the human race no longer exists." It was half question, half statement. She couldn't help but notice Maria's unsettled composure. Rose pressed on. "What happens if the nanorobots are removed from our systems? Is there nothing left of us? The human us? Are we mere shells for robotics?"

Maria shifted restlessly. "I'm not sure I'm the one to answer these questions, Rose, dear. And I'm not sure it's safe to even ask them."

"What happened to the king's wife? What happened to Queen Eleanor?"

If the other questions hadn't unsettled Maria, these questions certainly did. Pulling her hands away from Rose, Maria sat, head bowed, staring at her feet. "Without the nanorobots, we all die," she spoke so softly, Rose could barely hear what she said. "Queen Eleanor insisted on having the nanorobots removed. I'm not sure if her orders were carried out, but she disappeared one night, along with the royal yacht. It was only much later we heard bits and pieces of her rescue in Florida and her restoration to the Luthensteinian royal family. She lived out her life in an enclosed facility for the insane. Whether or not she was insane, no one knows for sure. But the stories she must have told the outside world would certainly make them believe she was insane."

"She lived a long life," Rose noted, her voice equally quiet.

"Yes. But what quality of life?" Maria stole a glance at her young charge. "Well," Maria stuttered, trying to find a way to explain herself. "You asked if we as humans were now doomed to be robots, controlled by the powers of the Atlanteans. At least, I believe that was the gist of your questions." Rose nodded. "We can still reproduce. Your baby brother is an example of our ability to continue conceiving. He is totally human. I think."

"Perhaps not," Rose suggested. "Perhaps not as much as you think he is. If he was taking nourishment from Mother while inside her wound, then it's quite conceivable that he inhaled, so to speak, some of her nanorobots."

"Oh dear!" Maria moaned. "You may be right. But there's nothing we can do about it. We are what we are, and we should be thankful to be alive."

"To what purpose?" Rose challenged. "What is it exactly the Atlanteans want from us?"

Maria pulled back and stood up. It was obvious from her rigid stance that she wasn't going to answer Rose's question. Perhaps she couldn't. Did the nanorobots control her mind as well? But, no. That couldn't be the case. If it were, Rose wouldn't be asking all these questions. She wouldn't be able to.

Releasing a deep breath, more intense than a sigh, Maria said bluntly, "You should rest. Sleep. Doctor's orders. Even with the nanorobots, you need your rest to fully heal." She turned her back on Rose and walked across the room, taking a seat far enough away to dodge the intense stares from her charge.

Rose wondered if Maria had the same thoughts and questions plaguing her mind, but was terrified to openly challenge the Atlanteans. Was it as dangerous as she was beginning to think? Seriously dangerous? Had the queen suffered immensely from doing just what Rose was doing now? Had others suffered as well? And to what purpose? Was it wrong to want some answers? She wasn't about to abandon the island and its people. Where would she go? If what the Atlanteans said was true, her home planet was totally immersed in water. All she wanted were some answers, to understand why she was here, why all the others were here. And why they were being kept alive for centuries. She always dreamed of a long life, but not as long as some of the people on Dulces Sueños Island had lived. Even Prince Edouard was older than a hundred. If her math was right, Edouard should be about 102. And the king would be 135. Neither looked as old as they really were. Far from it. She wondered how old Maria was, and, for that matter, Dr. Burns. Her parents should look as if they were reaching sixty. Instead, they didn't look a day older than when she last saw them when she was only four.

The jumble of questions swirled through her head, making her dizzy. She closed her eyes to sooth the tumble of thoughts. The next thing she knew, she felt someone gently nudging her shoulder. "Rose. Wake up." It was Maria. Rose blinked her eyes, wincing at the bright light. As Maria's shadow cleared, the older woman spoke, almost apologetically. "I'm sorry to disturb you, but Doctor's orders. I must wake you up to make sure you don't slip too far away that even the nanorobots can't revive you." The older woman tucked a hand behind Rose's shoulders and helped her sit up. "Here. Sip some water." Rose obliged and Maria carefully settled the young woman back onto her pillows. "Now sleep some more. It's the middle of the night. I'll be right here if you need me."

Rose didn't need urging. Her eyelids drooped shut and she slipped into a dark void of nothing. She woke again to see the light streaming in the window. Morning. Already. She yawned and stretched. She could feel a few kinks in her joints, but nothing painful. Slowly, she pushed herself into a sitting position, allowing her legs to slide over the side of the bed. Feeling a wave of dizziness, she paused. It settled quickly, faster than she thought it would.

"Those nanorobots," she muttered under her breath. Glancing around the room, she noticed Maria settled into the comfy chair by the bookshelf, an open book slipping off her lap. The woman was sound asleep. Convinced that the dizziness had abated, Rose pushed herself off the bed, straightening her legs until she was standing. No more spinning. No pain. A few jabs here and there, but nothing intense. It was a good sign. Carefully, she tiptoed toward the window, valiantly trying to be quiet as a mouse so as not to disturb her caregiver. She made it to the window seat and let out a sigh of relief as she settled into a kneeling position so she could look outside. Leaning over the cushions, she cranked the window open and rested her elbows on the ledge. Poking her head out, she breathed in the clear, fresh air. It felt so good as the whoosh of cold freshness reached her lungs. It wasn't bitterly cold. Merely crisp. An early morning cold.

After allowing the sun to soak warmth onto her face, Rose opened her eyes and took in the same sights she had seen the previous morning: fields of grain, paddocks of livestock and people starting their work day, all dotting the landscape, making it realistic. Satisfied that nothing had changed, she glanced down at the ground beneath her window: the patio where she was about to have tea and dessert with the king, the same patio where he had been on the verge of stating his intentions, too soon. Much too soon. It all came back to her in a flash. She had been startled. She hadn't expected a proposal, from a man old enough to be her great great great grandfather, from someone she had only met a few days ago. It was all too bizarre to comprehend.

She shook the cobwebs from her head, banking down the unwelcome memory. Blinking her eyes, she brought her thoughts under control and allowed her eyes to explore further. They settled on the stone steps, the ones she had fallen down, backwards, or so she had been told. There must be at least a dozen steps, all rough stone, sharp and hard. The doctor said she had rolled to the bottom. Smashing her back and head multiple times in the process. And, yet, here she was with hardly an ache in her body. The fall should have killed her. These nanorobots were powerful inventions. Scary and powerful.

"You're awake," Maria's voice pulled Rose away from the window and away from her memory of the night before. The young woman settled down onto the window bench, grabbing one of the cushions to cuddle, a protective motion she often resorted to when feeling unsure about things.

"Feeling better?" the older woman asked.

"Yes," Rose managed a faint smile of reassurance. "Remarkably so. Considering the tumble I took." She nodded toward the window, indicating the patio and offending steps below.

"Yes," Maria agreed, walking slowly toward the window. "Truly remarkable. But, then again, it's not the first time you miraculously survived near death."

"You mean when I was picked up off the beach," Rose noted.

"Yes." She took a seat next to Rose. "And then there was your allergic reaction to the initial insertion of nanorobots which also nearly took your life."

"What am I? A cat with nine lives?" The two women shared a chuckle. "How many more lives do I have?"

"Hopefully just this one." Maria reached over and took one of Rose's hands in hers. "And the nanorobots will ensure that it is a long one."

Rose groaned and shuffled uncomfortably. "I really don't like this sense of losing control over my life. Over my body. But it appears I have no choice."

"Not really," Maria agreed, giving her charge's hand a final pat before standing up and walking toward the bed where she started fussing with the covers, tidying things up. "There is no other choice. Not anymore. The world beyond is gone." She spoke quietly, almost reverently.

"But how do we know that for sure?" Rose asked. "How do we know the Atlanteans aren't feeding us another line, providing false images to make us believe what they say?"

Maria paused in her fussing and looked serious at the younger woman. "We don't. But others, humans, have ventured out to explore and bring back refugees. They have seen the destruction. There is nothing left of our planet. Except here. Where we are now."

"Couldn't the tales of explorations beyond be mere fabrications as well?"

"You're not a very trusting soul, are you?" Rose shook her head. "At some point in everyone's life, we have to let go and trust. The Atlanteans mean us no harm."

"So they claim."

Maria was quiet for a few minutes as she straightened the bedsheets. When she spoke, there was a serious tone to her voice. "You have no choice, Rose. Not now. You will come to understand and appreciate. In time." Glancing up from the sheets she was arranging, Maria attempted to hide her worries with a weak smile. "I know the king was hasty in his proposal. It startled you. But, you have to remember, a hundred years ago, Fred was told who to marry and the proposal was a mere formality. I know things have changed, even for royals, but, you know the saying, you can't teach an old horse new tricks." Restlessly, she ran her hands along the edge of the sheet she was holding. "It's no excuse; I realize that. But I thought you should understand where he's coming from. He believes he's done nothing wrong and he doesn't understand how he's offended you." Glancing up at Rose, she added, "I just thought I should mention that. Give you another perspective of what happened last night. Now," she forced a smile, "why don't you have a good, soaking bath and dress for the day. I'll have some breakfast sent up. You'll feel better once you're dressed and you've eaten something."

Realizing there would be no further revelations from Maria, at least for the moment, Rose agreed and made her way into the bathroom.

Chapter Twenty

Rose pondered Maria's words of wisdom while she soaked in the tub. It was true. A hundred years ago, when Fred had been king in his own country, he was told who to marry. Sometimes old habits die hard. She was smiling when she came out of the bathroom, dressed in a favorite sweat suit, warm, but not hot. Just comfy. She smiled to herself as she sat at the table prepared with her breakfast. Breakfast in her room was a godsend. Rose was hungry, surprisingly after all she had eaten the previous day and the shock her body had endured from the fall. It was a relief not to have to sit at the grand table next to the king. Maria's explanations had helped. Somewhat. But here she was referring to situations with classic sayings, much like Maria had done. How many more old sayings would pop into her head as the day progressed?

After breakfast, Rose slipped down to the conservatory. Maria had mentioned that the king wasn't in the castle. She would be alone. Music was her solace. She couldn't function without a good musical workout in the morning.

"Don't overdo it, Rose," Maria warned. "The nanorobots are still working on mending your body after last night's fall. Don't be hard on yourself if something isn't working quite the way you think it should."

Rose had brushed aside Maria's warnings, until she sat down at the piano. She started, as she always did, by working through her technical repertoire. However, after the third scale, the fingers in her left hand were cramping. She had heard of musician injuries that affected their dexterity and ability to perform. There were treatments and surgeries to fix most problems, and physiotherapy helped as well. Rose could only hope that her nanorobots would do the job of fixing her hands quickly and efficiently. Her right hand appeared to be functioning fine, so she decided to make this morning's workout a one-handed affair.

Finishing her technical warmups, she moved on to Czerny and took relish in fiercely attacking the right-hand parts of his Études. Starting with the simplest, she quickly progressed to the more difficult works. Some were mere technical exercises, but there were a few that boasted a modicum of melodic ingenuity. She enjoyed the melodious Études the most. After Czerny, she picked up the manuscript Amadeus had presented her the other day, the one he had just composed, or so he claimed. She had sight-read through the work under the maestro's watchful eye (and ear), as well as in front of a large audience. Now, alone, at least she hoped she was alone, she could take the piece apart and work on it diligently, one hand at a time. She worked through the right-hand part first, relishing in the melodic inuendoes, so typical of Mozart. After a thorough study of the work, she flexed the fingers of her left hand. Satisfied that they were working again, she started playing the left-hand part. She only made it about halfway through the first movement before the fingers cramped up again.

"Damn!" she exclaimed. "Damn! Damn! Damn!" She hoped no one heard her swearing. And so loud, too. But she was frustrated and she had to express her anger at the sudden onset of a disability. She had never been one to demonstrate patience. She could only wait so long. She needed her hands. They were her lifeline to the music that nurtured her soul.

Picking up the music, she shuffled it in order, and set it on the side of the music stand, stacking her Czerny repertoire album on top. With a final arpeggio across the keys, right hand only, she walked away from her beloved instrument. She couldn't take any more frustration. Not today. She merely ran her fingers lovingly across the surface of the piano, resisting the urge to return to it, to sit down and play. If she were to practice longer there was the risk others would hear her and come to listen. She wasn't up for an audience this morning. She wasn't ready to confront the king, either, for that matter.

She walked out of the castle via the conservatory's French glass doors. She made it across the manicured lawns and into the quiet woods beyond, intending to find her way to her parents' cottage. She thought she remembered the route Dr. Burns had taken her the previous morning. She was deep in thought as she walked the well trod paths. So, deep in thought, she was startled when a voice spoke, right next to her. Turning, she realized Helen was keeping pace with her.

The wizened Atlantean flashed a warm smile at Rose. "Good morning," she greeted the young woman. Rose studied Helen intently, trying to assess the woman's age. "I'm 3,851 years old in human years," the Atlantean responded, answering Rose's unasked question.

"Wow!" was all Rose could think to say in response. "How does that measure in your years? Atlantean years?"

"We don't measure years," Helen brushed off the question with a slight wave of the hand. "We are born. We learn. We grow. We work. Eventually we die. Although even death is not seen in our culture as the end as everything about us is re-used, or recycled as your Earth people would now call it."

"Even your bodies? Your soul? Your mind?"

"Yes, all of it," Helen responded in a simple, matter-of-fact tone of voice. "You Earth humans have begun the process, recycling organs to keep people alive. But you still have a long way to go." The two walked in unison, Rose massaging her left hand vigorously with her right as she kept pace with the Atlantean. "You are frustrated this morning."

"My left hand." Rose held it up in front of her face for closer examination. "I guess last night's fall injured it more severely than the rest of me. The fingers froze when I started playing the piano just now." She sniffled, barely holding her emotions in check. "If I can't play…" her sentiments were left dangling. She cleared her throat. "I am nothing without my music."

"Hmm! The nanorobots will fix it. Be patient."

"Not one of my strong points," the younger woman admitted.

"No, it isn't, is it?" Rose didn't answer. The two walked companionably in silence, each deep in their own thoughts. "You have a lot of questions, Rose." Helen finally broke the silence. "Some very challenging questions, shall we say?"

Rose didn't respond immediately. She kept her focus on the path ahead, maintaining a steady pace. After a few moments, she stopped abruptly and turned to stare at the Atlantean. "Is there a problem with asking questions?" she demanded, hands now on her hips. "Don't I have a right to know? Don't we all have a right to know? Why are we all here anyway? What is your purpose in keeping us alive when all the rest of our planet is gone? Or so you say."

"Believe me, Rose," Helen glanced calmly at the younger woman. "Your world is gone. All of it. And, believe it or not, our sole purpose is to help your people try again."

"Like after Noah's flood?"

"An apt comparison."

"But where?" the young woman challenged. "There's nothing left out there." She waved a hand aimlessly to dramatize her statement.

"We will find a place," Helen responded calmly. "Perhaps another planet."

Rose shook her head in disbelief. "You liken yourself to gods far too often," the young woman snapped a retort before she could stop herself.

Helen didn't even blink an eye, instead responding in a calm, controlled voice, "We are not gods, Rose. Your people presumed we were gods because they didn't understand the things we could do. You don't understand, so you're afraid. You challenge. You want to fight back, but you don't know how. Your thoughts are dangerous ones, Rose. Not dangerous from us. We will not harm you or prevent you from living your life and doing what you feel you must do. But if you continue on this rebellious path, you will only fire up more fear amongst humans, a fear that will turn violent and your people will do what they have done for centuries: they will fight to the death, to the complete annihilation of all humans." She paused to take a breath. "At least all Earth humans. We are humans, too, Rose. Did you know that?"

Rose shook her head, her mind a jumble of thoughts.

"We are humans, as you people on Earth call yourselves," Helen continued. "Many billions of your years ago, our ancestors settled on planets all across the universe. We progressed at varying stages, some, like the Atlanteans, becoming more advanced than others at a quicker pace. However, we all shared one common trait: we fought when angry, we fought when afraid. Even Atlanteans came close to extinction because of our anger and fear. As far as we know, we are the last of our people, as you are the last of yours. Believe me, Rose. We are only trying to help. We want all humans to survive and thrive."

"Then why all the mystery?" Rose challenged. "Why can't you answer my questions?"

"I think I have, Rose." Helen turned away and continued down the path.

Rose pondered the aged Atlanteans words before scurrying to catch up. "Wait," she called ahead. "Please. At least tell me why I'm here. Why was I chosen?" By the time she had reached the bend in the path, Helen had vanished from sight and Rose was alone again.

A voice shattered the void around her. "You were chosen for many reasons."

Rose glanced around her. There was no one else in the woods. Shaking her head in confusion, she scattered the cobwebs of convoluted thoughts from her brain. A few minutes later, she continued on her way to visit her parents. Perhaps they could shed some light on her troubled mind and the ever-growing list of unanswered questions. Or, were they all answered as Helen had suggested they were?

Chapter Twenty-One

"Rose," her father greeted her. "How good of you to come visit. Your mother will join us shortly. She's caring for the baby."

"She's up and about already?" Rose was surprised, assuming new mothers spent days in bed recovering.

"Of course." Dad gave her a look of surprise. "Women have been having babies for centuries, Rose. Women who worked the fields would stop long enough to give birth and then carry on with the day's work, baby swaddled to their bodies." He shrugged. "It's nothing unusual. Besides, with the Atlantean technology…"

"You mean the nanorobots," Rose concluded for him. Her father merely nodded in response.

Changing the subject, he said, "I was about to brew some tea. Would you care for some?"

"Yes," Rose forced a smile. She felt stiff, formal. She shouldn't feel this way with her parents. But, then, she had hardly known them before they were wrenched from her life. "Why did you agree to stay here, Dad? Why didn't you come home? We could have been a family."

Her father hesitated briefly as he led the way down the hall to the kitchen. "There really wasn't any choice, Rose. Once we were here and initiated with nanorobots and Atlantean theories, promises and plans, we couldn't leave."

"Why?" She was being insistent. "Wasn't I worth coming home to?"

"Oh, Rose." Dad put down the kettle he had just filled and walked over to her daughter. Taking her in his arms he hugged her fondly. "Don't ever think that. The Atlanteans promised to watch over you and that we would be together again. I believed them. I also believed their other promises and their plans for our future, for the future of Earth and the humans who inhabit it. We all have our talents, things they deemed necessary for this new world order. Your mother and I with our science and ecological training. You with your music. The king with his wisdom in kind and insightful leadership. And the list goes on. The Atlanteans chose wisely."

"But now there are others," Rose pointed out. "Refugees from the Armageddon. They weren't chosen."

Dad let out a deep sigh. "No. They weren't. And it appears that some of the refugees as you call them are none too happy to be here. I believe the king is over there now, at the refugee camp, trying to smooth things over. If anyone can do that, he can."

Changing tactics, Rose challenged, "Were you recruited, Dad?"

He started at the sharp question and the tone of voice that projected it. Gathering his thoughts, he pondered before speaking. "I suppose we were, in a manner of speaking. But not how you are interpreting it. Zeus approached me after a speaking engagement at the University of Toronto. Of course, I didn't know then about Atlanteans and the oasis they had created in the Bermuda Triangle. He introduced himself as Dr. Jones. I didn't question his introduction. He didn't give me an opportunity. He challenged some of the things I had shared in my presentation. Asked me and your mother to join him later for dinner at the Royal York Hotel in Toronto. I couldn't refuse. I loved that place. What a shame it's gone like so much else." He paused briefly, again seemingly absorbed in his thoughts. "Then, after dinner, he asked us if we would consider manning a research vessel in the Caribbean that summer."

"The ship that disappeared with you on it," Rose surmised, interrupting her father's dissertation.

He nodded. "He claimed it was to do research on the ecology of the region. He believed it was the source of all that was good on Earth and, if we wanted to save Earth, that's where we should start. He was very cryptic about it, but we soaked it all up. And who could refuse a chance to cruise the Caribbean on a private yacht? Because that's really what it was. There wasn't much in the line of research facilities."

Rose was about to question further, but a booming voice exploded through the house. "Dr. Bell. Your presence is required. Bring your daughter."

"Zeus." Dad put down the kettle he had filled and motioned Rose to follow him. "Probably another rescue mission. I wonder what it'll be this time. And why does he request your presence?" His question went unanswered. He poked his head in the bedroom to inform Rose's mother that they were off on a mission for the Atlantean leaders.

Dad returned to the kitchen a few minutes later to find Rose still standing in the corner, taking everything in. He nodded back toward the bedroom. "Go. Give your mother a peck on the cheek and then we must be off."

Rose hesitated briefly before doing as her father suggested. She walked into the bedroom, trying to keep sound to a minimum so as to not disturb her baby brother. "Good morning, Mother," she whispered.

"Off on your first mission, so I hear," Mother beamed at her daughter. "Do as you're told." Once a mother, always a mother, as evidence from the motherly instructions. "For your own safety as well as for the others. It's dangerous out there. Very toxic. The air. The later. Everything is toxic."

"Yes, Mother." Rose leaned in to give her mother the required peck on the cheek. "And how is my baby brother this morning? Have you chosen a name yet?"

Mother shook her head. "No name yet. That comes with the naming ceremony."

"I suppose that means the Atlanteans choose our names as well as dictating everything else about our lives?" It was more of a question than a statement. A challenge, in fact.

Mother didn't answer. She avoided her daughter's gaze and said softly, "Go now, Rose. And guard your tongue. Please. For all our sakes."

Rose tiptoed out, perplexed by her mother's parting comments. Why would Rose's comments affect anyone but herself? Was she putting her parents and her baby brother in danger by asking so many questions? Perhaps it was time to garner her concerns and merely observe. There was much to learn through observation alone. Besides, what choice did she have? There wasn't anything beyond the Atlantean domain. Not anymore. Or so she was told. Repeatedly.

"Come along, Rose," Dad was waiting at the front door. "Duty calls. We have some people to save."

That captured Rose's attention. "Really? Where?"

"Mount Everest," Dad declared. "It would appear a cruise ship of some considerable size grounded itself on the tip of the what had once been the world's tallest mountain. How it managed to keep afloat as long as it did is a real mystery. The ship is now totally buried under water. A few survivors escaped the sinking ship and are now clinging to the mountain tip. There isn't much time, I gather. The passengers and crew, those still alive, and there's quite a few, won't stand a chance in the toxic waters. Some did escape on lifeboats, I understand from drone footage, but the waves toed them under in seconds. Not a pretty sight. Others cling to what remains of the majestic tallest mountain."

Rose had to trot to keep pace with her father as he talked. She managed a question or two, but that increased the dissertation of details. "Toxic waters? The water that covers Earth is toxic?"

Dad shook his head sadly. "I suppose it shouldn't come as a surprise, Rose. Our people have polluted the waters for so long. But that's not the main reason for its current dangerous levels of toxicity. When the storms raged, the waters rose and volcanoes added their mix to the havoc of destruction, the nuclear industry world wide collapsed, leaking its heavy water. And then there were also the so-called 'safe'," and he air-fingered the quotations for emphasis, "nuclear waste disposal sites which are no longer, shall we say, 'safe'." He air-fingered the quotations again. "So much nuclear waste in the waters that encompass our planet. It's very heavy water."

"I gather there's no sea life, then."

Dad shook his head. "And the waste from the oil sands, the vehicles, ships and aircraft that were sunk. There are actually fires on top of the water in places. The water is that toxic, it's ready to ignite."

"I thought the Atlanteans had already saved the last remaining survivors," Rose spoke her thoughts as memories clouded her vision.

"They do continually claim to have rescued the last," her father admitted. "The drones can only cover so much surface area at a time. Just when we believe we have the last of the refugees, the drones discover a new group clinging to life somewhere on the planet. We keep looking, Rose. And hoping."

Rose shuddered. "Can we save the Everest survivors? All of them?"

"We'll try, Rose. We'll try." And he picked up his pace, leading the way to the opening they had traversed the previous day for the meeting with the Atlanteans. As he led his daughter inside, he motioned in a different direction. "This way to the launch pad. The Altantean airship is an engineering marvel, but even it has its limitations in this toxic world. Let's hope it does the job of transporting us safely to our mission and back."

Dad's hesitant tone unnerved Rose. Fathers, she always believed, were supposed to be sure of everything. Especially when it came to their family's safety

Chapter Twenty-Two

Rose didn't see the Atlantean ship on the outside. She followed her father through a maze of hallways and finally found herself in a room full of Atlanteans and humans, rushing about, fussing with what appeared to be equipment or studying images on consoles on the tables and larger ones along the walls. It was a busy, noisy environment. No sooner had she walked into the space, then a door whooshed shut behind her. She must have jumped because her father patted her shoulder briefly to offer some reassurance.

"We are about to take off," he said. "I have work to do. Find a seat. It may be a bit rough."

"The others aren't sitting," she spoke loud enough to be heard above the din.

"They're used to the ship and its movements." He pointed to a row of seats along one wall. "There are seatbelts as well. Sit and observe. Your assistance will be needed once we reach the mountain top." Before she could counter, Dad had all but vanished, weaving his way through the throng of bodies doing this and that.

Without a specific task to do, Rose resolved herself to take her father's advice. She sat in one of the empty chairs and pulled the harness, which constituted a seatbelt, around her shoulders and buckled herself in. As soon as the snap connected, a shudder ripped though the floor, rattling the walls. The standing bodies gripped something and braced for liftoff, if that's what was happening. She glanced at the large console across the room. It flashed images of what Rose believed were aerial views of Dulces Sueños Island. It was larger than she assumed.

The vessel appeared to be lifting much higher, as the island diminished in size. It broke through some sort of invisible barrier, a fact that was only evident by the rumble that shook the ship as if it had made impact. As they rose from the barrier, waters raged all around them. Even the ship was being washed with waves and splashes of water, making the image on the screen waterlogged and unclear.

It was dark out there. That was what registered most significantly in Rose's mind. It was extremely dark. Not long ago she and her father had walked through the fields, bathed in warm sunlight. Here, there was no sun. Even as they lifted above the highest wave of water, there was no light from the skies above. In fact, the darkness above blended with the darkness below, making no distinct barrier between above and below, sky and water surface.

"Why is there no sun?" she asked out loud, to no one in particular. She remained strapped in her seat while everyone else was bustling about working on the monitors and communicating with each other and presumably was base operations back on the island. "No sun!" she exclaimed, a little louder this time.

A body sat down next to her. She glanced over and realized it was the young prince. "Edouard," she rewarded him with a smile, relieved to have someone next to her. "I didn't realize you were on board."

"I always go on these rescue missions," he proclaimed. "I'm not sure if I'm any help, but the Atlanteans believe it merits educational value. Or something like that." He shrugged it off. "You asked about the sun."

"Yes."

"There isn't any sun," he answered blandly. "It's been dying for decades now and, as Earth was drowning itself, it lost considerable mass, making the gravitational pull between Earth and the sun almost non-existent."

"But we have sun on the island," Rose countered. "How is that possible?"

"With science, anything is possible," Edouard replied.

"So, there's no longer a sun circling planet Earth?"

"Actually, Earth always circled the sun," the boy explained. "Humans merely believed the sun circled Earth because of the changing times of daylight. But it's the other way around."

"Okay." Now it was Rose's turn to shrug her shoulders. She had never been attentive in science class and astronomy wasn't taught in any great detail. She was learning more now, through experiencing the Earth's sad demise, than she had ever learned in school. "So, if Earth is no longer circling the sun because the sun no longer exists, what is Earth doing? Is it in freefall through the universe?"

"Pretty much." The boy nodded.

"Isn't it bound to run into another planet, or sun or asteroid or something if it barrels through dark space?"

"It could and it probably will," the boy agreed. "Unless we, or the Atlanteans, can come up with a better option and put it into action. I think they're hoping its freefall direction will lead it to another sun in the solar system and set things right again."

"I gather there's a lot of conjecture, still, even on the part of these brilliant, ancient Atlanteans."

"There's always conjectures and theories," Edouard pointed out. "Until they are proven one way or the other, conjectures and theories are just that."

"Approaching coordinates," a voice rang across the room. Rose wasn't sure who it was, but it captured everyone's attention as eyes diverted to the main screen. Still gray and water splattered, an image started to come into focus, a ragged point ejecting from the water's surface.

"Mount Everest?" Rose exclaimed. "How is it possible that the world's tallest mountain is almost totally submerged?"

"Most of the planet is already under water," Edouard pointed out. "Mount Everest may have, at one time, been over 29,000 feet above sea level at its highest peak. That's much taller than the world's tallest building. Burj Khalifa, in Dubai, was only 2700 feet."

"And I suppose it's totally submerged."

"As are all the other tallest landmarks and buildings in the world," Edouard admitted. Standing up, he added, "We should prepare to assist. We will be taking on refugees soon. It's important we wear hazmat suits to protect ourselves from whatever toxins are in the air or on the bodies we bring aboard."

"Why would the refugees be toxic?" Rose asked as she unbuckled the unharness and stood up to join Edouard, who obviously knew where to go and what needed doing.

"I'm sure your father has filled you in on some things," Edouard spoke as he walked briskly toward a sliding door that continuously opened and closed with air-tight silence as people whizzed in and out of what Rose had accurately assumed was the control room, or the bridge, as it might have been called on the Enterprise. "He's quite the eco-engineer and his expertise is frequently called upon to solve issues relating to life sustainability."

"He did mention there was no more sea life," Rose admitted, almost having to trot to keep pace with the young boy. "Something about the nuclear waste making the water very heavy and dangerous. He even said the water could and might ignite into flames."

"It has in places," Edouard confessed. "And it might spread. Quickly. It's more vicious than any wild forest fires that have raged around the planet in recent years. But to answer your question about the refugees. They've been exposed since the beginning of Earth's destruction. Who can predict how toxic they are?" He shrugged and turned a corner, leading to another set of whooshing doors. They entered a large room where people were donning what appeared to be hazmat suits. Edouard picked one off the rack and handed it to Rose before reaching for another one for himself. "Here. Start prepping. There's no time to waste."

Rose had some difficulties with the suit, but Edouard was obviously experienced and was able to assist. They both finished snapping the helmets in place as a voice came over the air, "Prepare to board refugees." With no visual aids in the room, Rose had no idea what was waiting outside.

Edouard handed her a harness with a long line and they snapped it onto their gear, the other end already firmly attached to a rod that stretched the length of the room. "In case you lose your balance or fall upon leaving the ship," he explained. "Or, worse. We can always pull you back in."

The thought of sliding outside the ship onto a sinking mountain top, one that was extremely toxic, held no appeal. She wasn't sure she wanted to step outside. Surely there would be enough manpower, more experienced souls, who could manage the recovery from outside the ship. She'd much prefer working from the safety of the interior.

As the ship steadied its hovering position, the doors slid open. Rose gasped. What once had been a testament of humanity's ability to conquer nature, or, in other words, prove the prowess and expertise required to scale the world's highest, and most treacherous, mountaintop, was now barely an acre of jagged peaks. The snow that had capped the majestic tip was long gone, leaving behind barren rocks and a few scattered bodies of the remnants of the human race. Most of the figures lay prone, barely moving, bundled in the protective gear they had carried on a trek to the top of Mount Everest, the last trek. Others wore layers of light clothing, typical wardrobe of cruise ship passengers, for that's what they were. In the distance, the hull of what was left of the ship creaked and groaned as it lay precariously perched on one of the mountain's jagged peaks. These people had made it. There were others crying for help from what remained of the ship. But at what cost?

One hand shot up and waved them over; the others lay comatose. The patches of exposed skin were blackened, charred beyond recognition.

Rose was swept forward with the others, stunned by what she saw. She knew she had to help. If she could. She walked tentatively across the uneven surface, wary of the splashing waves all around, that drummed ever closer, ever more threatening. Crouching beside a figure, she noticed minimal movement, a chest rising and falling. Barely. "Over here," she called to one of the other suited people from the ship. Two figures appeared next to her, carrying a stretcher between them. With both ease and care, they lifted the figure onto the stretcher and then carried it back to the ship.

Rose moved on to the next figure. "Help me," a voice croaked from somewhere beneath the charred skin. It may have been a woman's voice. Rose didn't know. It was irrelevant. This person, male or female, needed help. "Water."

Rose gently grasped what she assumed was the person's shoulder, patting it lightly. "Soon," she said. "Soon."

Eyelids flickered and blackened bulbs appeared from the depths of the sockets. "I can't see," the voice crackled. "Why can't I see?"

Rose patted the figure again. "Don't try to speak. Help is here." She waved another stretcher bearing couple over and watched as they carted the figure off to the ship before moving on to the next person.

She didn't know how long she wandered the corpses and near dead, but she was startled by a tap on her shoulder. It was Edouard. "We have to leave. Now." He sounded urgent.

"But there are still more people to rescue," she argued. Waving toward the creaking hull of the ship, she added, "And what about those people clinging to the ship?"

"No time." He pointed off in the distant. Rose allowed her eyes to follow the direction he was pointing. She gasped. A wall of water was thundering toward them.

"That must be at least ten storeys high," she exclaimed.

"Higher," the young prince agreed. "Now. Back to the ship. There is no more time. When that tidal wave hits, there will be nothing left of Mount Everest. Or anyone on its peak."

"But…"

"No buts." The boy argued with the insistence and perseverance of a full-grown male. No surprise, Rose pondered, since in reality he was well over a hundred years old.

Reluctantly, she followed the others back to the ship, leaving behind the weakening wails of those they were leaving behind. She tried valiantly to block the sound, knowing full well that it would haunt her for the rest of her days. As she stepped over what appeared to be a large boulder, she felt something tug the leg of her hazmat suit. Glancing down at the resistance, she gasped at the sight of a sharp blade swishing back and forth in the air, mere inches from the leg that was being restrained.

"Help me," the boulder was a body. Charred so badly, the person, or what was left of him or her, blended into the rocky surface of the mountain top. It was amazing there was still life in the remains, and enough life to give strength to wielding a weapon.

Rose tried to pull her leg free as she felt her harness tighten to pull her back to the ship. She was now alone on the surface, alone with the remaining victims of this horrific tragedy.

"Rose. Come. Now." Edouard was calling frantically.

She tugged harder. The body held firm. She could hear a roar behind her. Turning, she realized her time was running out. The gigantic wave was almost upon her, almost at the base of the mountaintop. With a final tug, she managed to free herself, but not before the prone figure made a vicious final swipe with the knife, slicing through the pant leg of her suit, nicking the skin of her leg.

Blood oozed out as Rose, now free, was all but dragged onto the ship, the harness Edouard had insisted she wear tugging her forward ever faster, her lifeline to escape.

It was not without recourse. Water raged all around her, all around the mountaintop, splashing with a vengeance. Her hazmat suit sheltered most of her body, but the exposed leg, now bleeding profusely, was a prime target. As water made contact to her skin, she screamed. The burn was unbearable.

She felt a strong tug. Through the intensity of the pain that shot up her leg, she could sense being dragged aboard the ship. The knife-wielding body's screams were drowned by the sound of the tidal wave and the vicious splashing of the water as it lapped victoriously over the mountaintop. It was all drowned out when the doors whooshed shut with a vengeance, cutting her and the others off from the wave that pounded the ship's hull. The ship took off, upwards. Straight up.

She remained on the floor, blood splattering everywhere, her screams piercing the cabin. She attempted propping herself up to survey the damage to her leg. To no avail. She was weakening at an alarming pace.

"Medic," someone yelled nearby. It might have been Edouard. She really couldn't tell for sure. "Seal the room. She's been compromised." Rose thought she sensed someone applying pressure to her leg. Although her screams had lessened, the pain hadn't.

More bodies crowded around her. With eyes barely open, she recognized shadows, nothing more. Voices. No one identifiable. They were working on her, following medical procedures. "The leg is gone," someone stated bluntly, oblivious to the shock it would give the patient.

"Shh!" Someone shushed the whistleblower.

"Well it has," the same voice became argumentative. "She'll have to know soon enough. If she survives. The rest of the leg needs to come off." The authority in the voice suggested a doctor, perhaps even a surgeon.

Waves of nausea swept over the young woman. Her leg. Gone. The words ricocheted through her pain smattered brain. Her leg. Gone. All in a blink of an eye. All because she was trying to help someone else.

"Into surgery! Now!" The authoritative voice was fading. Rose felt her eyelids drop as if lead weighted them down. Then darkness.

Chapter Twenty-Three

Once again, the light was bright. Too sharp. Rose blinked her eyes, winced and blinked again. She didn't want to open them; she didn't want to feel the pain. Too much pain. Then the memories crashed back: the rescue on the mountaintop, the cut on her leg, the comments about her being compromised, someone saying the leg was gone.

"Gone!" she croaked, the intensity of her attempt to speak causing a coughing fit.

"Here," a soothing voice spoke nearby. A hand gently lifted her head. "Drink some water." She took a sip. Then another. Her mouth felt like sandpaper.

"Mother?" Her voice came out in a garbled growl, not intentionally, of course.

"Yes, dear. I'm here." It was her mother. She was here. Taking care of Rose as she should have been doing every time Rose had suffered a childhood ailment. But she was here now. And that mattered.

"What happened? My leg?" She winced her eyes open. Blinked rapidly and struggled to sit up. With her mother's continued assistance, she managed a half sit, enough to look down the length of the bed. "It's there. I can see the leg's form under the blankets. I don't understand. They said... Someone said... I heard..."

"It was gone, Rose." Mother helped the young woman lie down again. "The injury you sustained from a contaminated blade, then the rush of highly toxic heavy water. Frankly, dear, you're very lucky to be alive. Even the nanorobots can only do so much."

"But my leg." She shook her head and wished she hadn't as the room started to spin. She closed her eyes to allow the spiraling sensation to settle. When it had, she opened them again. Slowly. "My leg is there."

"It's complicated, Rose." Mother took a deep breath. "You've heard of cloning experiments to create an entire new life form?"

"Yes. You mean, my leg is cloned?"

"In a manner of speaking. The Atlanteans, with human engineering expertise, have managed to clone body parts. The nanorobots assisted in the healing process once the cloned leg was attached. You're good as new."

"Good as a robot," Rose muttered under her breath. "How much of me is real, Mother? How much of me is still human?"

Mother looked away and busied herself fussing with the bed coverings. "Not much, Rose. Not much." Her voice was little more than a whisper. "When Prince Edouard and his father, the king, found you on the beach, there wasn't much left of you. The storms and waves that cascaded and sank the cruise ship were fiercer and more toxic than even the Atlanteans predicted. And you were tossed around at sea, in that toxic water, for several days before your body entered the safe zone, what you knew as the Bermuda Triangle."

"But I was conscious, wasn't I? When Edouard found me, I spoke to him. I asked for water." Rose shook her head in confusion. "How could I not be complete when I was talking, communicating?"

"You recall the bodies you rescued off Mount Everest?" her mother asked with a forced calm.

"Yes. It was horrible. They were mostly charred and blackened. And yet they spoke. Some of them, anyway."

"That was you when you were washed ashore."

"But how?" Rose waved a hand to indicate the length of her body. "How is it that I'm whole again? Was it all cloning and nanorobots?"

Her questions were met with silence. Finally, Mother spoke with care, "Can't undo what's been done. At least your mind is yours and always will be. And your passion for music. You should be thankful for that."

Another question popped into the young woman's head unbidden. "How did I survive in the toxic waters for so long before being washed ashore?"

Her mother hesitated again before speaking. "You remember the time you were in the hospital with pneumonia?" Rose nodded. She had only been about six at the time. But very sick and Aunt Olivia had rushed her to the hospital, fearing that she might not make it. "Helen was there posing as one of your doctors. She managed to have a nanorobot injected into your blood stream. Just one, but it was enough to help you recover from pneumonia and keep you alive until you were washed ashore here.

Rose shook her head in disbelief. "I didn't react to that nanorobot," she noted.

"It was only one," her mother explained, "And the Atlanteans have been experimenting with different materials ever since. Unfortunately, the ones they inserted when you arrived here had something that triggered an allergic reaction, which they quickly assessed and resolved."

Rose was quiet, absorbing all the information her mother had provided. With a deep sigh, she spoke in a quiet voice, "Are we all robots?" Rose had to ask.

Her mother didn't answer. She stood up, gave her daughter a gentle pat on the shoulder and walked away with another soft comment, "I've already said too much."

Rose was angry. Confused, too, but mostly angry. How dare they, how dare the Atlanteans presume to recreate humanity? In their own image? But, as her mother said, what could she do about it? Was there any point in fighting? Any point in challenging what had obviously been done for centuries?

As the door closed silently behind her mother, Rose studied her surroundings, pondering her rabid thoughts. She was in her room, in the castle, the familiarity of her belongings providing a much-needed balm to sooth the young woman's troubled soul. At least her space was a constant. Or was it? Rose's eyelids drooped shut. Exhaustion won out. The next time she woke, she felt a gentle breeze flutter across her face. Someone had left the window open. It was fresh, invigorating. Just what she needed to get up and about again.

She pushed herself into a sitting position. Slowly. Relieved when the world around her didn't start to spin. Slipping her legs over the side of the bed, she breathed deeply. In. Out. Even if she was a robot, or at least most of her was, she was alive and she could feel and sense things and she could think her own thoughts.

"Now where did that come from?" Rose muttered under her breath. "Am I being coerced into accepting things as they are?" She shook her head. This time the room did begin to spin. Not overly unsettling, just enough to keep her rooted on the bed a few more minutes.

"My leg," she pondered, still muttering to herself. She pulled up the left pyjama pant leg and studied the bare skin. It was perfect, satiny and smooth. No indication of trauma. Had it been the left leg? Or was it the right one? She pulled up the right pyjama pant leg. The same: smooth and satiny, so perfect. Reaching down, she ran a hand up one leg then the other. There was no sign of trauma; no sign of injury or surgical procedures. And it felt like real skin. It wasn't plastic or tough as she would expect for a robot's skin. She shuddered. Was she really a robot? Or a clone? Or both?

She sat back and continued to study her legs for a few minutes, allowing the spinning to settle again. Bending over, then straightening up again hadn't helped her vertigo. When the spinning ceased, she stood up, slowly. The legs appeared strong enough. There wasn't any pain, either. It was as if nothing had happened. She slipped her feet in the cushy slippers next to the bed and puttered over to the open window. Leaning out, she breathed in more deeply, closing her eyes to savor the moment.

Noises below distracted her moment of reverie. Opening her eyes, she glanced toward the source of the noise and gasped. An entire army of people, well it had the appearance of being an army, was marching toward the castle, three and four abreast and a line that stretched as far as the eye could see.

"We want answers! We want answers!" the chanting cascaded across the expanse, sending shivers up and down Rose's spine. So, she wasn't the only one seeking answers. What did they want answers for?

Other voices added to the counterpoint: "We're not robots! We're not robots!"

And: "Give us back our bodies! Give us back our bodies!"

Someone in the troop must have noticed her leaning out the window. Soon everyone was pointing at her and shouting their demands even louder than before. The movement of human traffic picked up its pace as if it were charging her. They were throwing whatever they could find. Nothing came anywhere near the castle, but the impact was unsettling. Startled, she ducked back inside and pulled the window shut, latching it firmly.

"Rose," her mother's voice came from behind. "I see you're up. And you've noticed our protestors."

"Yes. What's happening?" Rose stepped back from the window ledge, wanting to put more distance between herself and the angry mob outside. "What do they want?"

"The same thing you want, it appears," her mother stated blandly. "They are from the refugee camp. Somehow, they broke through the protective barriers and they've been marching since dawn. Since the king has been their only contact from outside the camp, they're seeking him out for more answers. At least, that's what we are led to believe at the moment."

"But why are they so violent? Aggressive?" Rose's worried expression sought consolation from her mother. "Shouldn't they be satisfied with being rescued and safe from the Armageddon that has destroyed our world?"

"Are you?" Mother challenged her daughter, lifting one eyebrow to accentuate her question.

Rose was startled by the question. She had spent most of her conscious hours on Dulces Sueños Island asking questions, demanding answers. She hadn't received half the answers she requested and she certainly wasn't satisfied with the answers she did receive. And, now, to discover that she was mostly a robot and barely human at all, the questions continued to pour into her head, stewing up a storm of unrest and discontent. Perhaps she should be out there with the protestors.

As if to sooth her troubled thoughts, the cacophony from the protest, which had been intensifying considerably as the marchers approached the castle, came to an abrupt end. Silence ensued.

"What the…?" Rose didn't finish her exclamation. She hurried back to the window and, opening it, leaned out. The protestors were gone. "Where did they go?"

She glanced over her shoulder at her mother, but received no verbal response, only a shrug of the shoulders. "They did this, didn't they? The Atlanteans. They erased the problem. Is that how they deal with those who disagree? With those who challenge them? With those who dare to question?" She was spitting out a tirade of questions.

Her mother didn't answer. She merely stood complacently until her daughter settled down. Then she spoke. "We all make choices in life, Rose. When your father and I were shipwrecked and stranded on Dulces Sueños Island, we were given the choice to accept things and help prepare for a better world, or to return to the troubled one we left behind and face the consequences of our massive injuries."

"You could have returned to me," Rose spoke with a vengeance. "You had a choice and you chose to abandon me."

"No, Rose." Mother came over to the window and sat next to her daughter, taking the young woman's hands in hers. "Look at me, Rose." She waited until Rose complied. "We couldn't return.

Our injuries were too severe. We would have died. There was no choice to return to you. It wasn't part of the equation. We were allowed to monitor your growth and your successes and be the proud parents from afar. But we couldn't return to you. They promised us," she sniffled, took a deep breath and continued. "The Atlanteans promised that the day would come when we would be reunited. On this island. It was not an easy decision to make, Rose. We didn't like the idea of never returning to you, never seeing you grow up, graduate from high school and university, perform your first concert at Carnegie Hall. Life is full of difficult positions, but, if we had chosen to leave Dulces Sueños Island, we wouldn't have been able to return to you. We probably would have died before we reached the Florida coastline."

Rose sat in silence, pondering her mother's words. "But there's so much that isn't right here, Mother. How can you just accept it?"

"It hasn't been easy, Rose. No choice in life is an easy one. But at least we could continue our work, our research and hope that someday we could be a part of a better world, a safer, healthier world."

Rose glanced out the window, pondering the fates of all those rescued souls. The refugees who had denied what was offered. Their choices had proven fatal. Was she risking fate by asking so many damning questions? Should she accept what she has, her parents, her new baby brother, and make a new life for herself here on Dulces Sueños Island? A life full of music? And love, should she decide to accept the king's advances?

"Rose," her mother pulled her back from her inner conflict. "You have to decide. You have to make a choice. You have to stop asking so many questions. There is a lot to do in the days, months and years ahead. We have a lot to do to prepare for Novae Terrae. Whether it's here on what's left of planet Earth or on some other Earth-like planet somewhere in the solar system, we have to prepare to create the best world ever."

"But there's never going to be a perfect world," Rose argued. "Perfection doesn't exist."

Her mother shook her head sadly. "So true, Rose. But that doesn't mean we should just give up and not try. We're being given another chance. A chance to create a better world. All the arts have been preserved. The brilliant minds from across the centuries. Scientists are exploring new possibilities never before imagined. There is so much we can learn from the Atlanteans and so much we can share with them."

"I don't know, Mother," Rose spoke with a quiet, sad voice. "I really don't know."

Chapter Twenty-Four

"Come with me, Rose." Mother held out a hand as if requesting her daughter to take hold. "Come. I need to show you something."

"What?" Rose asked, hesitant. What more was there to know? What more did she want to know? "Where are we going?"

"To the library." Realizing her daughter wasn't going to take her hand like the child she was no more, she allowed the raised arm to drop at her side. Turning, she walked to the door and opened it. "Come."

They walked down the hall, but didn't descend the grand staircase. "Isn't the library on the main floor?" Rose asked as she continued to follow her mother.

"It's on every floor of the castle and many floors below," Mom explained as she opened a set of double doors at the end of the hall. "This is the main repository of every book, every bit of writing, every piece of music composed, every recording of the music, every movie or sitcom ever made. It's all here."

"And works of art?"

"Only reproductions and works created here on the island by the same masters."

She motioned her daughter into the room. Rose stepped inside the door and her eyes nearly popped with amazement. "Wow!" she exclaimed in awe. Her eyes drifted upwards first, taking in the tall domed roof, complete with marvelous stained-glass windows. Around the colorful dome were images of creation, not unlike the paintings that graced the ceiling of the Sistine Chapel in Rome. Now gone. Like everything else. But here were the images again. Bigger. Bolder. "Michelangelo," she whispered with reverence.

Rose's eyes dropped from the pristine ceiling art to the cavernous space directly in front of her, above her and way below as well. The walls were encased with dark wood framed shelves, the wood polished to a fine sheen. She wasn't familiar with the different types of wood, but she recognized quality when she saw it. Each shelf was stuffed full of books, with ladders on rungs to swing around from one shelf to another to allow a person to browse with ease. She stepped further into the space and leaned on the railing that ran around the circumference of the book-encased space. She looked up and she looked down. Everywhere she looked, there were shelves of books on multiple landings similar to the one on which she stood. There was more here than she would imagine existed even in the Library of Congress and the British Library combined, reportedly the two largest libraries in the world.

Niches between rows of shelves were garnered with classic sculpture, from ancient civilizations all the way forward to the modern world. Paintings graced paneled walls where neither books nor sculpture commandeered the space.

"In the lower regions are the ancient scrolls and maps, works in more fragile condition and in need of restoration and delicate care." Her mother had allowed Rose the opportunity to gaze in awe. Now she moved toward a staircase that led down to the next level and to another set of stairs that would lead even further down. "There are rooms dedicated to the preservation of original music manuscripts, as well as recording studios where music recordings are shelved. It's a massive collection of the world's greatest creative minds through the centuries."

Rose followed her mother, too spellbound to speak. She gawked at the contents she passed, the massive wealth of creativity. "Wow!" she finally found her voice. "Why wasn't I shown this before?"

"There was no need," her mother answered bluntly. "Now you need to see everything. To know and understand everything." She glanced back at her daughter as she made her way to yet another set of stairs. "Then you must choose."

"Choose?" Rose scrunched her forehead in confusion. "Choose what?"

"To accept and stay," her mother continued with her blunt, no nonsense tone of voice. "To challenge and refuse and be banished. Which, of course, would result in instant death."

"Do or die," Rose muttered under her breath. If her mother heard, she didn't respond. She merely carried on down one set of stairs after another, until they reached a base where the floor stretched from one end of the space to the opposite end.

A large table dominated the central space. Made of heavy wood and polished to a sheen, it was like any worktable one would find in the classic old libraries around the world. Rose wondered if that, too, had been confiscated for the Atlanteans use.

As if reading her mind, a familiar voice spoke from behind. "Yes. It came from the Bibliothèque nationale de France. In Paris. The other reading tables, or worktables came from other libraries around the world. We certainly didn't want to raise suspicions by taking all the tables from one library." Helen had been reading her mind. Rose was sure of it. "Yes," Helen quickly responded. "I do read minds. Nothing is secret on this island. Although, I do pick and choose whose mind to read. If I tried reading everyone's mind at once, I would have a cacophony of racket plaguing my brain. Even Atlanteans can only take so much idle human thoughts."

Rose turned to face the Atlantean. "That's invasion of privacy." She couldn't help herself. She could feel the anger reaching a boiling point. "Is there nothing I, or anyone else here, can do or think or speak without you or one of the other Atlanteans knowing about?" She glanced around the room. "Where is Zeus?" She noticed all the figures around the table, studying one document or another. She thought she recognized some of them: her father, of course, and the king. But Zeus was nowhere to be seen. "I haven't seen him since that meeting in your chambers, if that's what you call the place where we met. And, for that matter, where are all the other Atlanteans? Or, are you and Zeus the only ones?"

Helen looked visibly unsettled by Rose's questions. "You need to curb your curiosity, young lady," she snapped. "Zeus has other matters to attend to. As do the other Atlanteans." Glancing over Rose's shoulders, she addressed the young woman's mother. "Why is she here?"

"It is time," Mother responded. "She needs to know." She didn't elaborate, allowing the 'need to know' line to address a void Rose could feel closing in all around her.

The Atlantean gave a barely perceptible nod and took the lead, walking with a dedicated purpose toward the tables. She waved her hand in front of her face and holographic images appeared hovering over the table. All Rose could do was gawk. She had seen such things in science fiction movies, but to actually witness one in real life, blew away her mind. It was a multi-dimensional view of Earth, as if they were hovering over the planet from some distance away.

"Wow!" she mumbled under her breath.

"Pretty awesome, isn't it." The sound of the king's voice, near her ear, made Rose jump. She hadn't recovered from his unexpected attentions the other night. She wasn't sure if she could.

Taking a step away from the voice, Rose studied the hologram and listened intently as Helen explained what was being revealed.

"The world has been dying for centuries," the Atlantean spoke with assured confidence. "We plotted and planned and prepared for the inevitable, hoping to save as much of Earth's treasures and as much of human talents as possible. About six months ago, things started to decline rapidly." She waved her hands and images of roaring fires crashed around the space over the table. The sound effects and the sensation of growing heat swept over the people hovering around the table, observing Helen's display of recent history. Rose could feel beads of sweat forming on her brow. It was as if she were in the heart of the raging fires. "The Amazon forests. Within weeks, it was mere ashes and yet it still burned. You must have read or seen reports on the news." Rose nodded, not sure if anyone noticed her acknowledgement. "The entire continent of South America was on fire. Cities reduced to ashes in a matter of days." She waved her hands again and more raging fires burned before Rose's eyes. "Australia. Northern Spain. Germany. The deserted Nazi training camp, with all its buried explosives ignited and exploding from the intensity of the fire that destroyed everything in its path."

"It was like the Nazi terror had resurrected in full force." Rose found her voice, recalling the horrors she had seen recorded on live news broadcasts.

"Exactly." Helen stole a quick glance at the young woman, then waved her hands again. Another image, masses of people, an explosive force of its own. "Hong Kong." She waved her hands again. "Syria." And she took Rose on a visual tour of humanities destructive forces.

"Armageddon," Rose concluded, no further explanation required.

"And the volcanoes and the earthquakes, all around the world, explosive reactions from deep within the planet. And the tsunamis." Another wave of the hand. "This is your cruise ship shortly after it left port. The waters were already rough and more than a little choppy."

"I remember," Rose agreed. "The captain announced a slight change of route to avoid the more turbulent waters."

"It didn't matter much in the end."

The image that blazed in front of Rose's eyes showed the tidal wave that launched its attack on the cruise ship. The Royal Blue, huge even by cruise ship standards, was no match for the approaching wall of water. She watched in horror as the ship capsized, as people slipped into the waters and sank almost immediately, as lifeboats were lost before they even had a passenger secured in its hold. And then, as if a camera was zooming in, she noticed one figure being tossed about, a lifejacket barely keeping the person afloat.

Helen pointed at the image, then looked over her shoulder at Rose. "You."

The young woman gasped. She had no recollection of the events after she slipped off the slippery deck into the water. She didn't even remember the force of impact when she hit the water. All she remembered was sliding and screaming, "Aunt Olivia. Aunt Olivia." And the rest was a black hole of nothing until Edouard's voice reached out to her as she spat out a mouthful of sand. Then another black hole until she woke up in Maria's cottage.

Rose's eyes were glued on the image. Her, being tossed about and slammed against floating debris, remnants of the cruise ship, the lifeboats, other vessels and all manner of rubbish. Not to mention the cascading walls of water; she couldn't imagine, let alone recall, the sensation of being slammed, time and time again, by those huge waves. And, yet, she continued to float, her figure bobbing around, submerged briefly, then once again breaking the surface. Until, at last, the waters calmed.

"You've entered our space," Helen explained. "What your people call the Bermuda Triangle. As you can see," she waved her hands to bring the image of her figure closer, "you're barely alive."

"My skin," Rose gasped. "It's charred. Black. What happened?"

"Toxic water."

"It was toxic already?" Her father had mentioned the high toxic levels of the waters covering the planet, but she had understood that to happen after the mass destruction.

"Yes. The impact of those towering waves had already wreaked havoc with nuclear submarines and nuclear power plants across the continents, not to mention the so-called safe disposal sites for nuclear waste. Yes, the evolution of extremely toxic water was almost instantaneous." Helen waved her hand again and the image fast forwarded to the beach, to Edouard running toward a blackened remnant of a person, sprawled in the sand.

"There wasn't much left of me, was there?" Rose groaned. "Why did you save me?"

"We had always planned to bring you here," Helen explained. "Your parents insisted. It was part of their agreement to remain and help, to use their expertise to move our plans forward to a safer, cleaner planet than the one Earth's humans had rapidly destroyed. We had planned to bring you here well before disaster hit, but we hadn't anticipated the huge explosion at the Iranian nuclear plant which precipitated the chain of events that happened well before their time."

The images of Rose being carried off the beach, on a stretcher, was different from what she thought she recalled. She had felt someone carry her. She had assumed the king had picked her up and carried her to Maria's cabin. Studying her remains, she understood now that being carried in a person's arms was not practical, as the charred remains of her body would have crumbled and scattered over the beach.

She was shocked when she observed what must have been an operating room of sorts, where figured huddled over her and diligently administered care. What they were doing, she could only surmise. She gasped when she watched her body being lowered into a coffin-shaped container full of fluids.

Helen sensed the young woman's shock. "An incubator," she explained. "What remains of your original body continues to soak in the incubator in case we need to extract more cells to clone parts of your body. Like we did to replace the leg you lost the other day while on the search and rescue to Mount Everest. We did manage to preserve most of what's you. In fact, you were a bit of marvel in our scientific advancement into cloning technology."

"Glad I was able to be of service," Rose couldn't help but mutter under her breath.

Ignoring the snarky outburst, Helen continued, "The bones, except for the replaced leg, the inner organs and, of course, your brain, is all encased in the new skin that you currently sport. You are mostly you, the original you. The nanorobots have helped to heal and they also protect the new cloned parts from deteriorating, integrating the cloned and the real cells into a unified human form. You are the original you," she stressed again. "Pretty much, anyway."

"And the rest of me?" Rose asked bluntly. She was becoming more unsettled by the minute. Helen's discourse of what happened since Rose was tossed off the cruise ship was making things worse, not better. The tone of her voice bore evidence to her growing distaste.

Helen appeared oblivious to the younger woman's growing displeasure. She continued as if enjoying the opportunity to display the Atlantean advancement in medical technology. "You have been preserved." She waved her hand and the image that popped up made Rose choke with distaste.

"You have mummified my remains," she snapped, stepping back, wanting to put as much distance as she could between herself and the image, between herself and the Atlanteans. "I may as well be dead." She shook her head and waved her hands frantically in front of her. "No. Wait a minute. I'm already dead." She elbowed her way through the people who had congregated behind her: the king, her mother and father. "I'm done here!" she yelled as she started to run. "If I'm really dead, be done with me. Bury me. Bury all of us. There's nothing left of our world anyway." She was ranting, venomous spittle splattering from her mouth as she shared her thoughts. She charged to the nearest door, not knowing where it led as she was now several storeys below where she and her mother had entered.

Chapter Twenty-Five

"Rose," a voice pierced the stunned silence that engulfed the growing space between the woman and her adversaries. For that's what they were: adversaries. That's how she saw them. Even her parents. There was no one to trust. No one to understand. No one to care. They were all robots. And what of her baby brother? Was he real? Or another cloned implant to paint a pretty family picture?

"Rose," the voice called out with greater intensity. More insistent. Closer. As she barged out of the library, she felt a hand clamp over her arm, pulling her up short.

"No!" she screamed in protest. "No! Let me go!"

She turned to face the aggressor. "Your Majesty," she spat, recognition mixed with discomfort. "I suppose you still want to force your intentions on me, don't you?" More spittle flew from her mouth, splattering the king's face. She didn't care. Why should she? She was just a robot. They all were. Robots. Toys of the Atlanteans. Nothing more. She didn't bandy her words. With equal venom, she spoke through clenched teeth. "Perhaps it's my turn to force my intentions. Take this."

Before the king could respond, Rose had grabbed him behind the neck with both hands, pulling his face toward hers. She wrenched her lips against his, applying as much force as she could. Satisfied she had made her point, she stepped away suddenly and wiped her mouth with the back of one hand. "There. Now you have an idea of what it feels like to have someone else's intentions forced upon you. Though, believe me, I really have no intentions where you're concerned. I'm done. With you. With my parents. With them. With this." She was waving her hands frantically in the air around her, emphasizing her point. "In fact, I'm done with life. If this is life." She swirled around to take in her surroundings. "Then I want nothing to do with it."

She was about to storm off, but the king took her arm to prevent a dramatic exit. "You don't mean that," he scowled, pulling her around to face him. He now had both hands grasping either shoulder. He had a firm grip, but not a harsh one. "I want you, that much is true. But certainly not if you don't want me. I lost one love and I don't intend to lose another. My wife, my queen, I loved her, but she couldn't stand it here. She couldn't stand the way the Atlanteans manipulated and controlled everything and everyone. Me? I understand their purpose, their intent. I also realized I couldn't go back. Not to the plastic life I lived as a puppet monarch. For that's all I was: a showpiece to put on display when the need arose. And, we were all seriously injured and repaired by the Atlanteans, as were you. Leaving here wasn't an option. We wouldn't survive out there. Not without the Atlantean technology. And they weren't willing to extend their services beyond this island."

She could escape if she wanted to, but something was stopping her. And it wasn't the king. She glanced up at the man who held her, as if seeing him for the first time. Through frantic tears that now cascaded down her cheek, she studied Fred intently. As he spoke, from the heart, she saw another person standing there, one as lonely and as desperate as she was. "But your wife left. And she lived for many years off Dulces Sueños Island."

"Yes. So, I understand." He lessened his grip. "But what kind of life did she lead. I understand she was locked up in an insane asylum to live out her days. What kind of life was that? And she never got to see her son again. Or her husband. She was alone. More so than she was here on the island." He released his grip and started to pace. It was a large room, but nothing as grand and gracious as the library or any of the other rooms in the castle, for that matter. Rose had no idea where they were, though it was probably several storeys below ground as she and her mother had made a lengthy descent after entering the library.

The king continued to talk as he paced. "There's nowhere else to go, Rose. The world as you and I knew it is gone. Forever. We have to start afresh. We have to. For the sake of the human race. Or, what's left of it. We may never be the same humans we were before all this happened, but we are still human. And we have a responsibility to accept this gift from the Atlanteans, to start again and try to make a better world. It may not be perfect. We may not be totally human. But we are alive and we do have the opportunity to do something good for our fellow humans. That much I agree with. And, for that reason, I carried on, year after year, trying to make sense of what and who I was. I'm still trying to make sense of it. I had hoped to find a helpmate in you, one who could share my burdens. One who would understand my confusion. One who felt very much as I did."

He glanced over at the young woman who hadn't budged since he released her. She was studying him intently, a sense of calm descending over her tear-stained face, as the salty flow fizzled and ceased. Finally, she nodded. "Okay." She reached out her hand and he returned to her, taking the hand in his. "Okay." She sniffled. "But don't rush me on the partnering process. I was never very good with relationships. My life has always been my music. Nothing else mattered. Except Aunt Olivia. But she's gone now."

"They tried to save her, too, Rose," Fred consoled her.

"Did they?"

He nodded and forced a weak smile on his face. "Yes. They did. But her body was so badly damaged from the time being jostled at sea and the cancer that was already taking her life. Even Atlantean technology has its limitations."

Rose sniffled again. "I'm glad they at least tried. Thank you for telling me."

"And I will slow down my intentions." His smile broadened. "For now, can we at least be friends."

Rose returned his smile. "Yes." And she meant it. She still wasn't sure about being a robot, but perhaps over time, she could accept who she was now. And, she still had her music. "Can you lead me to the conservatory? I'm quite lost and I think I need some alone time with my music."

Fred tucked her arm in his and led her to the far end of the room. "Stairs or lift?" he asked.

"Stairs. I'll enjoy the exercise of climbing. How many storeys?"

"Ten."

"Ugh!" she groaned. Bracing her shoulders back, she allowed the king to lead her toward her music.

Chapter Twenty-Six

Rose followed the king through a maze of hallways, doors, up countless sets of stairs and along more hallways. Finally, she felt familiar with her surroundings, but she was convinced she could never find her way back to the auspicious library. At least, not the way they had exited.

Fred stopped and dramatically opened a set of doors. "Your conservatory, my lady," and he bowed quite formally. "I hope your music sooths your soul. I know it sooths mine."

As Rose stepped into the room, a shuddering shook the floors and walls around them. She jumped, grabbing Fred's arm for support. "An earthquake?" she gasped.

The king didn't have a chance to answer. An announcement came invading the space: "Atlantean One has landed. All hands to their posts. I repeat. Atlantean One has landed."

"Atlantean One?" She maintained her hold on the king's arm.

"I have to go. Quickly." The king gently released the young woman's grasp. "Atlantean One is one of the Atlantean's space ship, the one that explores the universe and reports back to home base. Which is here. On Dulces Sueños Island. Their recent mission was to find an Earth-like planet for us to settle and start a new life. I wonder what they have found."

"But I thought we were to renew life on this planet?" she half asked, but her question fell on deaf ears. Fred had left her alone in the Conservatory.

She had a choice. She could try to follow the king and find out what's really going on. Or, her preference, she could bury herself in the conservatory with music. She chose the latter. She would find out soon enough. At least, she hoped she would.

She walked slowly across the marble-tile floor, allowing the ambiance of the space to soak through her skin. That is, as much as it was her skin. She would have to stop thinking this way, challenging everything she did and felt. She was who she was. Human surgeons had been performing transplants for over a century, not just human organs, but limbs and skin as well. She would have to assume that this was no different, only higher tech with the nanorobots flowing through her system and keeping her well and strong.

As her footsteps echoed on the hard floor, the scents of the flowers that claimed every peripheral corner and crevice around the glass-domed space invaded her sense of smell. She breathed deeply. As well as the flowers, there was the sweet smell of fruits, mostly citrus. Her eyes roamed the circumference, savoring the colors as her aromatic senses devoured the scents. It was soothing. Calming.

By the time she had reached the piano, her piano, she was calm again. She had restored a sense of balance, a sense of ease with herself and with the world, what was left of it. As she took her place on the piano stool, she ran her fingers gingerly across the smooth, ivory keys, tainted yellow with age. She warmed up with some scales and other exercises, deciding as she played that this sense of place required, no demanded she perform works like Beethoven's ever famous "Moonlight Sonata" and a Canadian composer's piano solo that literally reached for the stars: "Leaping through the Stars". The ethereal quality of both works were deeply soul-searching and powerful expressions of the world beyond.

The soothing melodies of the Beethoven classic gave way to the hauntingly aspiring sounds of the universe. Rose played with her eyes closed, a smile warming her face. She knew these works by heart. They were her passionate release when the moment demanded passion and a sense of peace. She was so immersed in her music that the ear-piercing shriek that crashed through the castle and beyond had her jumping off the bench with shock. She managed, barely, to maintain her balance by grasping the side of the piano with one hand and the stool with the other.

"Rose." The king stormed into the conservatory. "I wanted to get here before you were startled, but I see I wasn't in time. So sorry. The Atlanteans are making ready to lift off post haste. Planet Earth, as we knew it, is long gone and readings from the center of the planet reveal a startling amount of built-up energy. To put it simply, Earth is ready to explode at any minute."

"But where do we go? How will we survive?" Rose let go of her piano and ran to Fred, seeking comfort in human contact. She couldn't help herself. He opened his arms and wrapped her warmly against him, patting her reassuringly on the back.

"There is little time for explanations," he said, his voice void of emotion in spite of the close contact with the woman he proclaimed he wanted to make his mate for life. "The exploration team returned with news of an earth-like planet. We'll settle there for now. Perhaps permanently if it works out. The shaking we felt earlier was the unsettled state of the planet's interior forces."

"Earthquakes from within?" she pondered aloud, pulling back from the embrace enough to glance up at the king's face. His look was serious, more than she had ever seen it before.

"Yes," he agreed. "And worse. The Atlanteans are now securing things in the castle and the university. Everything will be saved. Or, at least as much as possible. We are instructed to seek refuge in the tunnels below the surface. We must be strapped into harnesses before lift-off. Come. There's little time."

"But my piano!" Rose couldn't believe she was arguing about things when her life was in the balance. She glanced at the room around her and the gardens and land beyond the glass enclosure. Her eyes returned to the king. "Will everyone be saved? My parents? The refugees?"

"As many as possible," the king answered sparingly, his hesitation and bluntness suggesting that things were not quite as they should be.

"We're not taking the refugees, are we?" Rose challenged. "Why?"

"There's no time to argue, Rose." Fred forced a calm demeanor in the tone of his voice, but he was also being firm. He took her arm and led her from the conservatory. "Your parents and baby brother are on their way underground as we speak. Your piano and belongings are safe. We must make haste."

As she followed, reluctantly, the king's lead, Rose heard a whir all around her. She glanced back and noticed movement, what appeared to be filaments of plastic, or something similar, stretching across the expanse, wrapping things up in the process.

"Is that how they secure everything?" she asked, but received no answer. Fred was moving at a quick pace and she had to jog to keep up.

He led the way, down into the bowels of the castle. "This is the quickest way to the tunnel refuge," he explained curtly and picked up the pace yet again. "We must hurry." The noise around them was intensifying. "They're preparing for lift-off." He barged through one set of doors after another before finally reaching a room where others were hustling about, fastening themselves into seats lining the walls, much like in the drone they had taken to rescue survivors off Mount Everest.

"Rose," her mother rushed over and grasped her hands, her face looking frantic. "We were starting to worry."

"You're here," Dad appeared at Mother's side. "Come. Let's get fastened in. They're just about to lift off." As if on cue, a rumbling shook through the walls, the floors and everything not yet fastened down, rattled and shook with a vengeance.

Fred grabbed Rose's arm, Dad took Mother's and the four stumbled to the last remaining free seats and quickly fastened themselves in.

"Secure for lift-off." A voice bellowed through the air. Doors latched shut with a clank, filaments spread across the space, covering everything and everyone. Before the faces were submerged, facemasks dropped from the ceiling. Rose copied the others and positioned it over her face, breathing deeply and trying to relax. A shudder shook the floors, rattling the walls with a compelling force. Holographic images projected in the center of the room as voices updated the situation.

"Hull breech. Situation critical." The message was repeated several times as the room shook and rattled with a vengeance. The images projected what appeared to be explosions, flames of bright oranges, reds and yellows flashing around the holographic space.

"Planet Earth has imploded. Situation critical."

Rose observed the panicked looks on the faces of those strapped in around her. She mirrored their sentiments. As the filament covered her entirely, the images, noise and shaking were obliterated from her consciousness, and she felt herself floating in a black void.

Chapter Twenty-Seven

She hadn't realized she'd dozed off. Or perhaps the air filtered through the facemask, which was no longer on her face, had drugged her to sleep. Or was it really sleep? Yawning, she wrenched her eyes open, taking in the surroundings. At first, confusion set in. Then she remembered the course of events that preceded her being strapped in. The filament that had covered her and everything and everyone else, was rippling its way back into some sort of hold, leaving the space uncovered and free. People around her were starting to stir.

"Rose."

She glanced to her left and noticed her mother unfastening her straps. She looked to her right and saw her father doing the same thing.

"Have we landed? On the new planet?" she asked no one in particular. Recalling her last conscious experiences, she queried, "What happened when we were lifting off?"

The king was already up and about. He walked over to her and extended a hand. "Yes. We have landed. The lift-off was rough as Earth self-destructed before we were totally disengaged. There was some damage to the Atlantean vessel, but, as you can see, we are all well and safe. Come and see for yourself. Our new home. Our new planet. Novae Terrae."

She unfastened her straps and stood up, a little shakily as the blood rushed from one end of her body to the other. She had no idea how long she had been strapped in, drugged and sleeping. Like all the others. She took Fred's hand, more to steady herself than anything else. "Start walking," he advised. "It helps get the blood flowing and you'll get your sense of balance again in no time. We haven't been cleared to exit the ship yet, but we can study the surroundings from the drone images coming in."

"Is everything intact?" Rose asked as she followed Fred's lead. She glanced around, taking in the people she knew and those she hadn't yet met. Everyone was busy with their assigned tasks. Or, at least they were making themselves useful. She suddenly realized the only person she couldn't account for was the price. "Where's Edouard? I don't see him."

The king was calm in his response, as if he were accustomed to not seeing his son for long periods of time. "He's been busy," he reassured her. "He enjoys working with the Atlanteans and, with his brilliant mind, I do believe he's an asset to their work. And, yes, I believe everything from Dulces Sueños Island is intact and as it should be. We had to leave behind some of the coastal lands and the area beyond the island. The protective dome was failing fast and there wasn't time to launch the entire Bermuda Triangle, as we knew it."

The doors whooshed open and then shut again, attracting Rose's attention. As if he knew he was being talked about, the prince marched into the room. Taller. Older. A mature young man, now. No longer the gangling boy he had been when Rose last saw him. "Father," he greeted the king. "Rose." He favored her with a warm smile. He walked toward the center console. "I presume you've watched the holos of our hasty exit from earth?" he queried. People all around nodded their heads in response.

Edouard waved his hands and a holographic image appeared before them. "Earth," he explained. Waving his hands, he copied the actions of Helen who had magically made holographic images appear and disappear with a mere hand motion. "As seen from one of the Atlantean's scout ships in outer orbit. There," he pointed and the image zeroed in. A halloed blob was ejecting from the flaming globe that backlit its ascent. "We are just lifting off." Everyone watched in awe as a large blob detached itself from the main core of the planet, like a living cell dividing itself and setting the new growth free. As their spaceship moved further away from the planet and appeared to be completely free of attachment, a huge explosion erupted from Earth's core. The ship was spun away at a ferocious speed, whirling about as if losing control. The images continued to focus on the planet as it self-imploded in mere minutes. And then there was nothing. "The end of Earth," Edouard spoke with solemn reverence.

Flicking his hands again, another image appeared. Another planet. "It looks like pictures I've seen of Earth, taken from space," Rose observed.

"Yes. It does," Edouard agreed. "But it's not Earth. This is the planet we're on now. And this," he flicked his hands again, "is the landscape around our landing place."

The others were speaking amongst themselves, marvelling at the images they were seeing. Edouard shushed them and zeroed in on an image outside their spaceship. "There appears to be some sort of settlement nearby." He returned his attention to the king. "Look."

The image before them depicted lush green fields lined with tall forests, not unlike something one would expect to find on Earth. The old Earth, that is. The one that had existed before the events leading up to Armageddon. The sky was clear and blue and there were picturesque mountains in the distance.

Waving his hands again, Edouard brought the image into sharper focus. "There." He pointed at a compound of temporary structures, cooking fires burning at various intervals and, in the distance, what appeared to be Earthling spaceships.

"Can you zero in on the space crafts at the far end of the compound?" Rose asked.

Edouard complied.

"Airforce One," Rose uttered the words she read off the side of the largest craft. "So, our illustrious president is already here, with his equally illustrious set of cronies." She couldn't keep the disdain from her voice. "How many other political forces managed to escape before the world came to an end?"

"So far, we have only stumbled across this group," Edouard confessed. "But we haven't yet scoured the entire planet. It's quite possible there are Russians and Chinese trying to set up base camps around the planet."

"Just what we need," Rose groaned. "A new beginning with old cronies to insure another sad demise of humanity." She felt like pacing, but she couldn't drag her eyes from the images before her. "How did they get here? And so fast?"

"I would hardly say it was fast," Edouard admitted. "The Atlanteans had intel that space craft were exiting Earth's atmosphere at least a month before the cataclysmic chain of events leading up to Armageddon."

"They must have their own intel to know so much so far in advance." She wrinkled her brow, concentrating on a memory that was buried deep. It came to her. "Now I remember. There was a launch, or several launches around the world, about a month before my aunt and I boarded the cruise ship. I was performing at Carnegie Hall. The president was supposed to be there with his wife and aides. I was excited at the thought of performing before the president. I had performed for royalty in the past, but the excitement of performing before a world leader never dulled. Then he didn't show. I didn't know until after the performance. Very disappointing. Fake news was all over the media claiming the president had been kidnapped by aliens. I guess they weren't far off the mark. He wasn't seen in public again. And then the world ended. They knew." She pointed an accusing finger at the hologram. "They knew. And I wouldn't put it past them to have had some involvement in the chain of events precipitating Armageddon."

"Look," the king interrupted Rose's ramblings, pointing to a trajectory of vehicles heading their way. "Our presence has been noted and they're coming to investigate."

"Hardly a welcoming committee," Rose pointed out, shaking her head in disgust. "They're fully armed and ready to shoot first, ask questions later. Earth human political forces, no doubt."

Fred cleared his throat, avoiding comment, keeping his eyes glued to the holographic images.

Edouard broke the stalemate. "There's Zeus and Helen," he pointed as two figures were seen exiting what must be the dome enclosure of the Atlantean vessel.

"They're alone," Rose noted. "Unarmed. Is that wise?"

Others had gathered around the group, anxious to witness the interchange that was about to take place. Rose was comforted to feel her mother's arm tuck into hers. She leaned in for warmth and comfort, suddenly realizing that someone was missing. "Where's my baby brother?" she asked, glancing with concern, first at her mother, then her father. "I haven't seen him since the day after he was born."

Mother answered with a nod toward a group of young people standing at the edge of the observers. "Over there."

Rose allowed her eyes to follow her mother's direction. There were several youths gathered together. None of them were newborns, that's for sure. "But they're all so big. They must be at least seven or eight years of age."

Mother chuckled softly. "Babies grow quickly, don't they?" She patted her daughter's arm. "I'll explain later when I introduce you to your brother. We named him Philip. We were in an extended period of stasis in space. Several years, in fact, Rose."

"Years?" Rose gasped, confusion etching across her brow. "But I thought..." She pointed to the images. "And what about them? How did they manage to find this planet? To travel here? And they appear to have only just arrived. At least very recently."

"Shh!" Edouard shushed them. She wasn't going to get her answers yet. But perhaps the others didn't know any more than she did. "They are about to make contact. Audio should be on soon and we can listen to the interaction."

"Greetings Earth humans," Zeus's voice came across loud and clear. He held up his hands, palms forward, to demonstrate his peaceful approach, unarmed. The manned vehicles and the people on board were not so peaceful. The guns lowered, eyeballing Zeus as their prime target.

One man, probably a general, stood up in the lead vehicle. He was armed, sheltered with what appeared to be bullet-proof gear, and he was surrounded by armed men and women (it was difficult to ascertain which gender from the images projected) at the ready. "Greetings," he called out in response, his voice booming with a challenge not demonstrated in Zeus's greeting. "How do you know we are from Earth? And what rights to you have to this planet we now claim to be Earth Regenerated. In other words, our new Earth."

"I had not realized there were claims made on this planet." Zeus kept his voice calm. Controlled. "We have only just arrived, as you see." He paused briefly, presumably for dramatic effect, allowing his eyes to roam across the expanse of armored vehicles. "Your machinery is from Earth," he answered the other question. "And Air Force One emblazoned on your spacecraft suggests a political force from Earth."

The general nodded. "Then who and what are you?"

"I am Zeus and this is my daughter, Helen. We are in charge of this spacecraft that brought us from Earth." He waved his hand slowly behind him to indicate the craft. He kept his motions to a minimum to avoid alerting the armed force that he might become hostile.

"Zeus," the general chuckled. "As in the god Zeus?"

"One and the same," came the blatant response. "Though I'm not a god. I'm an Atlantean. I do have Earth humans on board, those we Atlanteans have rescued from Earth before it self-destructed a few years ago."

"That's one way of putting it." The general fidgeted, generating a sense of unease, as if he didn't know what to ask next. "How many humans on board? And what do you propose to do with them?"

"Perhaps first we should learn who you are," Zeus countered. "I have told you who I am and now it is your turn. And then you may take me to your leaders."

The general grunted and held his head even higher, staring down on Zeus from his lofty perch on the vehicle. "I am General Smithers. In command of the President's armed forces on Earth Regenerated."

"And who is this President?" Zeus asked.

"President Edwin Jones, formerly of the White House in Washington, D.C. on Planet Earth. We evacuated all important personnel when the situation on Earth looked dire. We had expert advice on these matters."

"Is President Edwin Jones the one in charge?"

"No. That would be Hera and her advisors, Echidna and Typhon." It was hard to tell for sure, but it was almost as if General Smithers was enjoying himself, perched in a command pose, surrounded by armed forces and sharing details of his change of command.

There was a noticeable gasp from Helen. Even over the hologram, it was audible. "Mother?" she half-whispered.

Zeus appeared noticeably shaken. He quickly glanced at his daughter, most likely his piercing gaze a silent command to silence her. Returning his attention to the general, he queried, "My wife is here?"

"Oh yes! Your wife." He almost sneered. "She has been with us for some time, now. I believe she was secretly hoping you'd show up one day. And now," he waved a hand dramatically. "Here you are." He bellowed a throaty, bland laugh.

Back in the console room, Rose whispered, "Is Hera really Zeus's wife and Helen's mother? And who are those other two he mentioned?"

"Rose," Edouard shook his head in feigned disbelief. "Don't you know your Greek mythology? Hera is Zeus's wife, but she was so jealous of her husband and was easily swayed by evil forces to go against him."

"And those other two are the evil forces?" Rose asked.

"Echidna and Typhon are monsters born in the bowels of Planet Earth." Edouard seemed please to be the one sharing his extensive knowledge. After all, over a hundred years of reading and studying was bound to make a person very smart. At least, one would think so. "They were a persistent thorn in Zeus's side, always trying to overthrow him. Until he and Helen took their Atlantis and hid it in the Atlantic. What happened to Hera and the other two after that, is not really known, but obviously they are alive and well today and still wreaking havoc."

While Edouard was explaining in brief terms the characters been thrown into the equation, Helen had turned around and vanished inside the Atlantean ship. Zeus, alone, marched toward the armored vehicle. "Take me to Hera," he commanded.

The general had the look of a man ready to argue, but then thought better of it. "At ease, men," he commanded and the weapons were lowered. "Hop on board, Zeus. I'm sure your wife," and he spat the last word, "will be pleased to see you. After how many years?"

Rose wasn't sure if she heard right, but it sounded like Zeus muttered, "Not enough, years, General. Not enough."

The holograph fizzled out. A collaborative sigh was exhaled, as if everyone watching had been holding their breaths.

"We have work to do," the king commanded. "Rose, Edouard, let us go to the castle and make sure everything is as it should be."

"The castle?" Rose queried. "Really? It's here?"

"Of course," the king responded, making a hasty exit through the doors and into the corridors beyond, Edouard merely a step behind. Once again, Rose had to trot to keep pace. The last thing she wanted was to be lost in the tunnels and corridors beneath what had been Dulces Sueños Island.

"How much of the island is here?" she asked, but her question fell on deaf ears. She would find out soon enough.

Chapter Twenty-Eight

Rose was amazed at the condition of the castle. Everything was as they had left it; the protective filament coverings had obviously done what they were intended to do. The plants were as alive and vibrant as ever, as if they, too, had been put in some stasis condition to preserve them. Even her treasured piano was safe, secure and in pristine condition, complete with the last piece of music she performed sitting on the stand ready for her to sit down and tinkle with the ivories again. And she would. Soon. But there were things to do first.

She dashed up to her room. All was in order. She ran her finger along the surface of several treasured possessions as she made her way to the window. Opening it, she leaned out and was pleasantly surprised to find the castle gardens below in immaculate condition and the fields beyond teaming with life and activity. Much as it had been before they left Earth.

Closing her eyes, she breathed deeply, allowing the air to circulate throughout her body, refreshing her both inside and out. She could sit by the window all day and soak in the sights, sounds and smells with great contentment.

That is, until the peace and tranquility was shattered. Yelling and screaming from the rooms below filtered up to her open window.

"What right does she have to invade my life again?" It was Helen. Rose couldn't recall Helen ever yelling before. Something had surely riled her up. "She left me centuries ago and now she wants to re-enter my life as a beloved, caring mother!"

It didn't sound much different from the accusations Rose had hurled at her own parents. Only, they had left her decades prior to their reunion, whereas with Hera, it had been centuries.

The yelling continued, but Helen's voice became less distinct. Anxious to be privy to further details, Rose pulled the window closed and made her way down to the main floor, following the sound of voices. It was coming from the library. Unsure whether or not she should barge in, Rose stood in the entryway, debating her choices.

"You may as well come in, Rose." The king's voice bellowed his command to enter. She was unsettled to realize her presence had been so quickly observed. She walked toward the assembled group which included the king, Edouard, her parents, the doctor and Maria. And, of course, Helen. They were all seated around the long table that was piled with books and papers left behind from the previous work being done. Everything had the appearance of normality, as if nothing had happened to take people away from their given tasks.

"You should be part of this counsel," Helen spoke more calmly than she had sounded mere minutes earlier. She pointed to a vacant seat at her left. Rose sat. Then Helen continued. "He's wired, so to speak, so I've been listening in. Hera claims she wants to reunite with both Zeus and me. After all these years! All these centuries! We didn't even know where she was let alone if she were still alive. And now this! How did she know we would join her on this planet? How did she know?" Helen's voice was rising by the minute, returning to its confrontational, frantic tone from earlier.

"There must be a spy in our ranks," the king stated what must be on everyone else's mind. "But who?"

"What else has been said?" Rose asked. "Did Zeus discover who all these people are? They must be imbedded with nanorobots like we are. Is that possible?"

"Very possible," Helen agreed. "Nanorobot technology was well documented amongst Atlanteans. But to think that Hera and her evil minions made use of it, is unsettling, to say the least. Who knows what monsters they managed to recruit, or worse, create!"

"Why?" Rose challenged. The same question she frequently asked. "Why all this struggle for power? What is the purpose? For what possible good?"

"Only for the good of those who achieve such power," her father answered blandly.

"Shh!" Helen held up a hand to silence further discussion. She was listening intently to something, presumably Zeus.

"They're wired, so to speak, through their minds," Mother whispered in her ear to explain.

After a few minutes, Helen glanced around the table, her eyes ablaze. Rose wasn't sure if the look was one of anger or fear. Perhaps both. "They're coming here. My father is bringing that woman here!" she spat the last few words. "And who knows who else will be in her entourage! I must prepare the security. Maria, will you advise the kitchen staff? Doctor, would you be so kind as to find the butler and prepare him? The rest of you, please dress appropriately for a formal state dinner. There isn't much time. We must be ready for anything and everything." Before anyone could question further, Helen had whirled in a blaze out of the library.

Chapter Twenty-Nine

Rose had been to state dinners before. Usually as the guest artist of the evening. Never as a guest at the head table. She wasn't sure if she'd be at the head table this time, but she was prepared nonetheless.

She chose her wardrobe wisely. In spite of the years in outer space transit, in stasis mode, she was pleased to note that her body hadn't changed in size. There must have been nourishment fed to her and the others while in stasis. And there were the nanorobots, too, of course. She chose a long, silky dress that slipped nicely over her curves and hugged her with comfortable confidence. It was her preferred outfit for performing – light and cool. Although it hugged her body, it felt like a second skin, moving with ease whenever her body moved. Sleeveless, it left her arms bare, free to perform. With its curved neckline, her neck was bare, exposed, but not too revealing. The royal blue color suited her. It brought out the creamed tone of her skin which glistened with perfection.

She wasn't sure if she'd be called to perform during the evening's events. She had slipped into the conservatory after Helen's hasty departure and worked her fingers to the bone, quite literally, going through an acceptable repertoire so she was prepared if asked. She was pleased that her fingers followed her commands and her workout at the piano didn't show any neglect from lack of practice.

Years. Some had said they'd been travelling through space for years. And, yet, it felt like only yesterday when she last sat at the piano and played through her favored repertoire. It was difficult to imagine being held in stasis for years, floating through space. It was unfathomable. What other explanation was there?

Studying her reflection in the mirror, she huffed with frustration. It wasn't right. Incomplete. She fumbled through her jewellery box, looking for something special to wear. Her neckline was too bare. Empty. And her ears begged for something dangling from their lobes. There had to be something suitable, but not too ostentatious to complete her wardrobe. Her grandmother's jewels, perhaps. Even if they were only costume jewellery, they would add just the right amount of pizazz. Of sparkle.

A knock on the door disturbed her ponderings. "Yes," she called out.

"The guests are arriving." It was the king. Rose opened the door and took a sharp intake of breath. Fred was fully decked out in his kingly wardrobe, complete with epaulets, gold braid, pristine white gloves, medals and all the paraphernalia that marked Fred as royalty. He wasn't Fred anymore. He was the king. And, he really was a handsome king. With or without his fine dress and fancy ways, he was a man that attracted attention. Rose could feel herself falling for him. Unaware of the affect he was having on the woman, Fred rewarded her with a warm smile that sparkled its way to his eyes. "Would you do me the honor of accompanying me to dinner and during the discussions to follow?"

She returned his smile, rather more timid than she cared to admit. "I am honored, kind sir." She gazed into his eyes and felt a moment when similar emotions reflected back.

"And would you do me the additional honor of wearing these." He snapped his fingers and an aide appeared at his side, liveried in formal attire as well and carrying reverently a black velvet cushion, on which lay the most exquisite necklace and earring set that Rose had ever seen.

"Oh my!" she gasped, one hand flying to her chest. She didn't know what to say. Should she accept? Would it mean she was accepting him as well? Would she really object to accepting his advances, his proclamations? With a fluttering heart, she was no longer sure what she thought, what she felt. She reached gingerly toward the proffered display of glistening jewels. "I would be honored to wear these, Your Majesty." She dipped a slight curtsy, aware that her formalities had been lax.

"Allow me," the king removed his gloves and placed them across the aide's arm before reaching for the necklace. Rose motioned him into the room, leading the way to her vanity where she sat and glanced at her reflection. The king had entered behind her, carrying the necklace with care, his aide two steps behind. Rose lifted her hair, allowing ease for the placement of the jewels on her neck.

"These were my great, great grandmother's," the king spoke quietly. "They've been handed down from one generation to the next. Only to be worn on special occasions and by someone very special. The Atlanteans managed to rescue these as well as many other of my family treasures. As they did for you and many others. I can only hope that this will be the first of many occasions when you may choose to wear these treasures."

Allowing her hair to fall back into place down her back, Rose was speechless. She didn't know what to say. She merely repeated herself. "I am honored, Sir." The necklace felt cool against her skin, but the sparkle reflected the gentle curves of her neckline.

The king snapped his fingers again and the aide bent over Rose with the cushion still bearing the earrings. Rose selected one and, with care, fastened it to her ear. It wasn't meant for pierced ears, having a screw fastening device that she hadn't seen in years. She tightened it on the earlobe, just tight enough to hold without pinching. Then she took the other earring and placed it on the opposite ear. Finished, she took a minute to study her reflection. With the king standing over her, a hand now fondly resting on one of her shoulders, she felt complete. For the first time in a long time, if ever, she really, truly felt complete.

Rewarding the king with another smile, projected through her mirror image, she said softly. "Thank you."

He returned her smile and gave his head a slight nod. He retrieved his gloves from the aide and pulled them on before waving a hand to dismiss the man. "Now. We really must go and greet our guests."

Rose picked up her own gloves and pulled them on. These had been her grandmother's and she enjoyed the sense of wearing the long, elbow-length gloves at any formal gathering. Standing up, she took the king's offered hand and followed him out into the hall and toward the head of the grand staircase.

The tone and volume of the conversation below was vibrant, animated and, at times, not so pleasant. Its mumbled version that met Rose's ears made no sense in spite of its volume. But it stopped, abruptly, when she and the king made their appearance at the head of the stairs leading down to the grand hall. They paused briefly to allow the silence to be complete before taking the first step down. They descended the grand staircase together. As a couple. The gathering of Atlanteans and humans, both theirs and Hera's, gazed up in awe at the regal pair making their grand entrance. Even Hera, for all that Helen had described her to be, appeared to be impressed.

Rose, head high, regal in her stature, felt as if she had found her calling, her place in this new world. She glanced across the sea of heads, recognizing some, including the General who had interacted with Zeus earlier. Most of the assembled she didn't recognize. There were still a lot of people from Dulces Sueños Island whom she hadn't met. Seeking someone familiar, her eyes finally landed on a huddled group. She had found her parents. They were both rewarding her with a satisfied smile. Beside them stood a young man, vaguely familiar. He looked like her father, with a twinkle in his eye that was definitely her mother. Was this the baby brother who had so quickly grown up?

They had reached the bottom step and came to a pause. Edouard marched forward and bowed to his father. "Your

Majesty," he gave his pier due reverence. The others in the room copied his example, bowing or curtseying in the king's honor.

There was a round of murmured *Your Majesty's* as the king took his cue to lead the way through the throng of people which parted in a grand wave of humanity and Atlantean, much like the Red Sea had parted for Moses. The king came to a stop in front of Helen and Zeus. He gave them a brief nod and then turned his attention to Hera and the man standing next to her.

Zeus spoke, "May I present my wife, Hera." Surprisingly, the Atlantean executed a very graceful curtsey, showing unexpected obeisance to the king.

The man next to her bowed his head slightly, speaking before he was formally introduced. "I used to be the President of a great nation," he said. His voice had a southern tang to it. "But never once did I receive the welcome we just honored you with. Very impressive entrance, I must say." Turning to Rose, he greeted her, "Rosalind Melodious Bell. I missed your last concert. For which I am very sorry. My wife was furious. But we had to leave. Not just the country, but Earth itself. Very dramatic."

"Mr. President," Rose smiled demurely, keeping her voice steady. "And where is your wife? Perhaps I could honor her with the concert she missed."

"That would be nice," the President agreed. "Only she's not here. She chose to remain behind. She thought my scheme to evacuate Earth a little farfetched, to say the least. I had to leave. I'm a leader and my presence on this new world was essential."

"And how many other leaders are there?" the king asked.

The President merely shrugged his shoulders. "I really don't know if there are any others. There was talk of the Russians and the Chinese and some Mid-Eastern countries making their own attempts to evacuate. Earth's final demise was expected. We were at the ready. Who knows for sure how many actually got away in time? Or, if they did, survived the lengthy stasis as they journeyed across space." He shrugged again. It seemed to be his character trait: shrugging. "But we're here. All of you and all of us. With you, dear king, as a picture of leadership and me actually leading, we'll make a great team."

If you could cut tension with scissors, it would crackle. Rose could feel Fred tighten his muscles in the arm she grasped as he clenched his fist. She could see Zeus's and Helen's eyes alight with fire. Hera merely smiled coyly.

What was she up to? Rose pondered.

Ever the diplomat, the king gave a slight cough to break the tension. "I do believe, Mr. President, that we have a lot to discuss. But perhaps that can wait until after dinner."

As if on cue, the butler appeared at the end of the hall. "Dinner is ready, Your Majesty."

Fred nodded his head in response. "Shall we?" he tilted his head as if not expecting a response. He was in command and he was making a good show of proving it. Turning with ease, Rose's arm still grasped under his, he led the way to the dining hall.

"Amazing how they can serve a grand meal when they have only just landed on the planet," the President could be heard grumbling from behind. "This is really a virtual Garden of Eden. Astonishing! I wonder what other marvels they have hidden and ready for us to confiscate."

Even Rose bristled at the last comment, as she sensed Fred tighten his grip on her arm.

The seating plan was well thought out. The king sat at the head of the table with Rose to his right. Hera sat around the corner of the table to the king's left, with Zeus at her side. The President was opposite Hera, on Rose's right side. The male-female alternating pattern continued the length of the grand table. Once again, Rose marveled at all the material possessions that had survived the extensive voyage across the universe, only to be set out so soon after they landed.

"This place is a marvel, really," the President spoke softly, close to Rose's ear. She shuddered at the breath that rippled across her neck. "Lovely jewels, by the way. Am I to understand that you and the king are a couple?"

Rose didn't respond. She hadn't decided yet and she wasn't about to let this parasitical politician be privy to that fact. She forced a smile, one that didn't reach her eyes.

"Ah!" The President was, if nothing else, rather astute. "Then there is time for a wily, old man like myself?" He lowered his hand to his lap and, a moment later, Rose felt it resting on her upper leg.

She brushed it away, but it returned a moment later. She brushed it away again. "Really, Mr. President. That is highly inappropriate."

He huffed. "Well, you can't blame a man for trying. The pickings are rather sparse around here." He turned his attention to the soup that was being placed in front of everyone simultaneous, as if orchestrated by a grand conductor. Rose and the President were not the only ones to admire the broth: its appearance and the aroma that seeped into the air with the steam. "Amazing! Hard to believe you were in stasis for how many years?"

"Three," Edouard volunteered from where he sat further down the table. His glance wandered from the President to Rose, a note of concern evident in his eyes. It was also territorial. He had obviously witnessed some of the forward advances the President had made toward Rose. His protective stance bordered on more than mere compassion. Was Edouard vying for her attentions in a way not so different from his father's? Now that he was full-grown, he possessed the body of a man not much older than Rose, in spite of the fact that he had lived for over a hundred years. It was quite possible he was enamored with the idea of seeking Rose's attention.

"Three!" the President exclaimed. "I would have thought you'd still be eating vacuum sealed rations. You've only just landed and already you have the resources to provide a healthy soup. Not to mention whatever else is on the menu for tonight's meal. Truly amazing!"

"Actually," Helen spoke up. "Most of what we're using is vacuum sealed, dried foods. Not rations, as you describe it. We were prepared for the inevitable. We do have most of the animals and natural vegetation and plants from planet Earth. We saved and protected at least of pair of each."

"Like Noah's ark," the President chuckled at what he assumed was a joke.

"Not so different," Helen agreed. "Though considerably larger."

"Well, with all these preserved treasures from Earth." The President paused briefly to sip his soup, allowing his unfinished sentence to hang on the already tense situation that was mounting by the minute. "Mmm!" he gave a satisfied groan. "Delicious. I do believe you have enough space and rations here to house us all. It certainly would be beneficial all around and safer than being out there, faced with the dinosaur-like monsters that lurk around after dark."

"Dinosaurs?" Edouard exclaimed; the child he once was reflected in the excitement evident in his eyes. "Wow! I'd love to see those."

"Not up close," Hera warned. "They've already feasted on some of our crew."

"We've probably landed on their nesting grounds," Edouard suggested. "Or their hunting territory. They wouldn't like that."

The President shrugged. "How were we to know? Besides," he sipped more soup. "We're here now and we're in charge. Isn't that true, Hera? We can take over this place you call home and rule it as we ruled Earth."

"And destroy it as you destroyed Earth?" Rose couldn't help herself. She never could abide pompous politicians, especially those who believed they were the gods of the universe and deserved to be treated as such.

Her brash comment was greeted with stunned silence. The President lowered his spoon and reached across to pat Rose's hand. "Now, now, little lady. We did nothing of the sort. Earth destroyed itself. All part of the natural course of events."

Rose was steaming. "Like the nuclear waste, the nuclear power plants, the nuclear submarines – and all the other toxic polluters that made the Earth uninhabitable?"

"The rising waters did that, my dear. The nuclear pollution happened after the waters rose."

"The nuclear pollution has been going on for a lot longer than that." Rose placed her soup spoon on the plate underneath the bowl, allowing it to make a bit of a clatter. "Those so-called 'safe'," and she air-waved the quotation marks, "disposal sites were hardly safe. The so-called 'safe'," and she air-waved again, "nuclear power plants were anything but safe, forever leaking, causing cancers to those who lived nearby and the heavy water waste was mounting at an alarming pace. The public outcry and protests fell on deaf ears. Those with the power to do something," and she pointed deliberately at the President, "those who could change things, make our planet safer, healthier. You did nothing! Absolutely nothing! You pontificated at election time and that was about it."

The king cleared his throat, putting down his spoon with more care than Rose had done. He nodded to the servers and the soup bowls were removed, replaced by a hot dish that might have passed for chicken and vegetables, only its wrinkled texture and discoloration was evidence that it was anything but fresh. It smelt good, though, but Rose no longer had the stomach to eat.

The king took charge of the conversation. "I think it would be best, for now," he spoke calmly, with a diplomatic ease of someone who was raised to be a leader. "I think it would be best if we finish dinner peacefully and parted ways after dinner. Now is not the time to have uninvited guests staying over."

The President, as dramatic as Rose remembered him from news reels on Earth, tossed down his napkin and stood up abruptly, pushing the chair back with such force it toppled over with a crash. "I think not." He nodded to the end of the table. "General. I do believe it is time to take control."

General Smithers, following the order from his Commander in Chief, stood up abruptly and ordered the men and women in uniform, all seated around the far end of the table to take up position. There was a cacophonic clatter of noise as chairs shrieked across the floor, some toppling over like the Presidents. The uniformed personnel quickly took up position at random intervals around the room.

"Well." Hera dabbed her lips daintily. "I guess dinner is over." She stood up gracefully. "My dear Zeus," she nodded at her husband and then her daughter, "and Helen. I am taking over as of this minute." Standing up with grace, unlike the raucous movements of the others, she flickered her eyes around the table, taking in the people on both sides of the confrontation, rewarding each with a forced smile. Her eyes came to rest on the general and she gave him a nod.

As if rehearsed to perfection, General Smithers removed the gun from its holster, something he had deviously camouflaged under his uniform. His men and women did the same and the deafening sound of cocking guns shattered the room.

Zeus cleared his throat and stood up. "I am afraid, my dear Hera, that you are the one who is mistaken. Knowing full well your notoriously devious nature, I was well prepared for your arrival." He took his time to glance around the room. "I feel bad that the chefs went to so much trouble preparing a fine meal. Perhaps my people will enjoy it after your people have left. If not, the pigs will feast tonight."

Hera laughed. It was a bitter, sharp laugh. "We're not leaving, Zeus. We are taking over your little compound here." She inched closer to her husband and spat in his face, viciously jabbing a finger in his chest to emphasize her point. "You have lost."

"No, I don't think so," Zeus countered, not flinching a muscle as Hera's spittle dribble down one cheek. "General Smithers. You are free to fire your weapons. However, you will soon discover they are useless. I have jamming devices in my compound, as you so eloquently call it." The general clicked his gun and growled when nothing happened. He attempted to throw it across the room, only to find his limbs were weakening and he barely had the strength to raise his hand, let alone his arm.

Zeus glared at his wife. "Gentlemen," he called out in a booming voice and the servants who had served them the soup stepped forward, shadowing each member of Hera's armed escort. "And, dear Hera, the soup was tainted with gelsemium, a mild version and only enough to make your people ineffective in physical combat. Oh, don't worry. My people are unaffected. Their soup was untainted. We had the seating plan carefully arranged." He gave his wife the smile of sweet victory.

"Our nanorobots will take care of that!" Hera spat her retort with spittle projectiles splattering at will.

"I think not." Zeus was sounding a little too smug. "Your scientists never did learn the full details of our advanced nano technology. In other words, your nanorobots are inferior to ours." His eyes narrowed as he glared down at his wife. "I've had you read for centuries, dear wife. I have always known your devious side. You may have thought you were able to manipulate me with your charms. But that ability ended centuries ago."

Before Hera could offer another retort, the king stood and took command. "Well, then." He glanced at the President with disdain. "If you are finished fondling my first lady, perhaps you would care to take your minions and leave our compound. Our people will see you out."

Chapter Thirty

It all happened so fast. One minute Rose was challenging the President, accusing him of being abusively destructive to the natural environment and its people, pointing out that he was not welcome in this new world. The next minute, he was ordering his troops to take defensive action and prepare to attack. It was the classic Greek legend, the Trojan horse approach to infiltrate the enemy camp inconspicuously.

Hera was next to take control, ordering weapons drawn. Zeus countered her threat with one of his own. He was obviously not one to allow the hornet's nest that surrounded his wife to attack what he defended: the world he had worked so hard to build up. In other words, Zeus was no fool.

The general aimed his weapon at Zeus and pulled the trigger, but nothing happened. His shooting hand lost its grip and the weapon shattered on the dishes at his place setting before he froze, visibly losing control of his body. The other armed personnel followed their leaders, their weapons, useless, dropping from their hands before they, too, were paralyzed.

King Frederick made the final stand, ordering his guard to remove Hera and her blight, jammed weapons and all. The armed guard was lifted, one by one, and carried into the hall where carts awaited to truck them out of the facility. Only Hera and the President remained, stunned, but not as aversely affected by the poison. Hera was led out first, stiffly, but managing to efficiently shrug off the escorts who attempted to take hold of her.

The President had made one final play as he was escorted around the head table. He reached out to grab Rose, to use her as a hostage, bait, to kidnap her. Who knew his true intent? He was abruptly stopped by a charge of energy, like a lightning bolt.

The onlookers watched in awe as the spark of energy sizzled up the President's offending arm, causing his entire body to shudder. Pulling his hand back, he retreated, as did the energy charge. Then Fred grabbed his arm, clenching it in a vice grip.

"No more!" King Frederick announced in a barely controlled voice that begged no argument. "She is not yours for the taking."

The President grimaced, glaring at the king. "We're not done here yet!" His tone of voice was a snarl. Very precise. Very forced. He was roughly man-handled and forced from the room. The silence that ensued was deafening in its absence of sound. The room felt like a black hole, if that was possible.

All the while, Rose remained seated, frozen in a daze. As did the others. All were intent on watching the drama unfold and play itself out. The blight removed, the castle and grounds locked up tight and secure, the king resumed his seat. He snapped his fingers, easing the mounting tension. The staff sprang into action, removing the dishes from the now vacant seats, as well as the soup dishes from those who remained. The next course was placed in front of each occupied setting, as if nothing had halted the appropriate course of serving a formal dinner.

"Eat up, everyone," the king commanded, picking up his utensils and digging in. "No point in putting good food to waste. It's been a long time since we enjoyed a meal like this." There were some muffled chuckles at Fred's attempt to lighten the situation.

The main course, what appeared to be chicken cordon bleu, was followed by a platter of dried fruits and petit fours, the latter obviously having been frozen for some time. Sweet, delicious, with a light flavor of freezer burn. Just a hint.

Rose glanced across the table at Edouard. He was enjoying his food, especially the sweets, as much as he had when he was younger. Which really wasn't all that long ago.

She felt a nudge on her elbow. "Eat," the king commanded in little more than a whisper.

She favored him with a smile and a slight shake of her head. "I couldn't possibly eat any more. I'm quite full. It was a fine meal. My compliments to the chef. Or chefs as it may be." She glanced over her shoulder at the head waiter who nodded in acknowledgement. The compliments, she knew, would find their way to the kitchen.

Conversation was stilted, to the point of being almost non-existent. The meal finished, everyone made their excuses and departed, leaving the king alone with Rose. Even Edouard had chosen to make his exit. He was more reluctant to leave than the others. Rose wondered again if he really did harbor intense feelings for her. She still couldn't get past thinking of him as the young boy who had rescued her from the beach only a few years ago. This ageless and quick aging process facilitated by the nanorobot technology made life confusing at best, complicated at least.

"Shall we?" Fred stood and extended his hand toward Rose. "Perhaps a walk on the patio would be nice?" Recalling his last fumble of pressing his feelings too soon, he quickly added, "I promise to be on my best behavior."

Rose chuckled softly as she took his hand. "I guess I won't be performing this evening. The guests have all left."

"You can perform for me anytime." Rose blushed. The king was teasing her, and she didn't mind. In fact, it felt comforting.

The pair left the dining room, taking a more circuitous route that led through the conservatory where they exited the French doors onto the patio. It was a clear night. Or, at least, that was the impression given by the protective shield of the Atlantean space craft. The stars were starting to appear, in patterns unfamiliar to Earthling stargazers, and there were two moons instead of one.

"Interesting," Fred glanced skyward. "Two moons. And more stars than I have ever seen in my life. Impressive." He didn't wait for Rose to respond, pulling her to the patio wall and taking her in his arms. "I know I promised not to be too forward, but I can't help myself. And I feel that this time is different. I sense you have feelings for me, feelings you didn't have on the previous occasion."

The flush that crept up her neck and absorbed her cheeks sent sparkles to her eyes reflecting the shining jewels in the royal necklace draped around her neck. "Yes," she whispered. "I do have feelings for you."

"Dare I hope that we can become a couple and share the role of ruling this new world as king and queen?" he asked.

"Are you asking me to marry you, Your Majesty?" She fluttered her eyelids coquettishly. This was so unlike her. She had never flirted before in her life. Certainly not as blatantly as this. Was it the nanorobots again taking control of her feelings and her actions?

"I do believe I am." The king slowly, majestically, bent down on one knee, still holding Rose's hands in his. "Rosalind Melodious Bell. Would you do me the honor of becoming my wife?" He kissed her hands gently, his eyes locked on hers, pleading, hopeful.

"Yes," she whispered in response.

Fred stood up and took her in his arms. As his lips approached hers an unholy screech wrenched through the air. Not one, but many.

"What the…?" The king didn't finish his exclamation.

"What was that?" Rose cried, jumping back in shock.

The screeching continued. Intensified. Then stopped abruptly, leaving behind an eerie silence, more painful to the ears.

"I don't know, but I believe we're about to find out." He stepped away as footsteps thundered toward them.

"Your Majesty." The Captain of the Guard barged onto the patio. "There has been an incident at the President's compound." He spoke in spasms, gasping for breath. "A lad pounded on the entrance, demanding assistance. I followed Zeus's orders to keep things locked tight for the night and not let anyone in. Particularly no one from the President's compound." He gasped and coughed.

The king, impatient to hear all, urged him to continue. "Carry on."

"We didn't let him in, Your Majesty," the captain explained, his breathing slowly to a more normal rate. "But he continued to pound and call out for help."

"Did he say anything?" the king asked.

"Yes," the guard replied. "From what we could understand, he was telling us that the President and the compound had been attacked by those giant dinosaurs they talked about earlier. The compound is totally destroyed and, from what the lad said, there are no survivors. He didn't look so good himself and I'm surprised he made it as far as he did. He was all bloodied and gored. And then, in a flash, he was gone. Picked up by some huge beast and devoured."

"You could see all this?" Rose finally spoke, shock making her voice thin and shattered.

"Yes. There are cams all around the Atlantean craft. We saw it all. Too much. I've sent out drones to observe the damage. I didn't want to alarm you unnecessarily. It might have been a scam after all."

"Yes, indeed." The king nodded in agreement. "Carry on."

"We sent out some drones and should have some images to study," the captain explained. "If you'd care to join us in the library. Zeus and Helen and the others are already there."

"Very well. Lead on."

"Fred," Rose whispered, "I mean Your Majesty. What does this mean? Will we be able to remain on this planet? Is it safe to inhabit? Safe to build a new world?"

"I don't know, Rose," the king had the pained look of one who was uneasy with the sudden, unexpected turn of events. "I really don't know. What I do know is that this space craft is not fit to journey any further. At least not in its current state. In fact, it might never be."

"What about the Airforce One crafts?"

Fred merely shrugged his shoulders. "You're assuming these creatures have left them intact. Besides, we have no way of knowing how close is the next inhabitable planet. We may just have to remain here and give it our best shot."

"You and me together," she smiled grimly. "Without the President. Without Hera."

"Yes," he returned her smile with a little more warmth than she expected. "You and me together. As it should be."

Epilogue

Ten years later

It hadn't been easy. There were times when Rose and the others thought they wouldn't survive. Somehow they pulled through. Discovering the destructive nature of the giant dinosaur creatures had been unnerving. Even the President's finest space vessels were destroyed. Learning later that Zeus had used all his powers and those of the other Atlanteans to eradicate the creatures from the planet had been unexpected.

"They were Hera's creation," he roared before the battle. "Giant robots with endless power and energy. She took her own minions, Echidna and Typhon, and refitting them with powerful nanorobots that took control of the creatures they invaded, recreating them into creatures far more evil than Echidna and Typhon had been in real life. And they turned on her. It would appear they were incensed when Hera and the President failed to take control of our little oasis. They cornered them at their weakest, before the effects of the numbing gelsemium herb the chefs added to their soup had worn off. Fitting that her own creation would serve against her and destroy her forever."

If humanity could take away one lesson from this incredible journey, Rose often thought over the years, it would be that technology was no toy and should be used and treated with care and respect. Next time they might not be so lucky, without Atlanteans to fight their battles.

Many died in the battle against the giant robot creatures, including Helen. Zeus held on a little longer, but his injuries were too great. He was rather old by human standards. He had doled out what advice he could before he breathed his last, knowing that he really couldn't control the entire fate of humanity. It was a lesson he had difficulty accepting, even after centuries living on Earth.

Rose married the king shortly after the final battle, having received Zeus's blessing with his final breath. They had two children and were expecting a third. Rose settled easily into married life and motherhood, accepting graciously her new role as queen consort. Though, music remained her one true passion.

The protective shields of the Atlantean craft slowly evaporated – quite literally. The castle, the university and the grounds that had once been Dulces Sueños Island remained. Although the land that had carried them to this new planet might support the human population for a few generations, many felt the urge to move beyond the confines, to explore and establish their own domains.

Edouard was one of these. The night before he left, he sought Rose out. "I can't stay here any longer, Rose," he spoke softly, a tone of sadness evident in his voice. "Or perhaps I should call you, Mother, since you became my step-mother when you married my father. I had once hoped, if I grew up fast enough, which the nanorobots helped, you might look upon me as a possible suitor. As a grown man, however, I realized that would never be the case. Your heart has always been with my father. I was only fooling myself in thinking you might feel something for the one who found you on the beach."

"My little hero," Rose smiled fondly, reaching out to the young man, who, in appearances, could pass as someone her own age. "I am sorry you feel you must leave. I will miss you. We have become great friends."

The prince cleared his throat. "We shall write. As all good friends do. We'll set up a regular courier system to exchange missives."

"We shall write," Rose agreed, biting her lower lip to stem the flow of tears that threatened. Too many changes. Too many people leaving. "Someday, you will find your life's partner. As I have found mine." The hug and embrace that followed was marred by tears shed on both sides. The formal farewell the following morning was more subdued.

Edouard realized he would never be king. At least, not at Dulces Sueños, which is what the people started calling the remains of the Atlantean outpost. He took a number of followers, including a few artists and scientists, and wandered into the uncharted wilderness, recording their findings and sending back regular reports. He did eventually settle down, about a five-day hike from Dulces Sueños. He built his own castle, which, surprisingly by all accounts, looked very much like his father's.

The Atlantean drones were used to scour the planet, but no further evidence of human life was found. There was plenty of space for everyone: lots of room to grow, to start fresh, to create a better world.

The nanorobots that kept everyone healthy for a long life started to lose their effectiveness with the loss of the Atlanteans who had created and understood them best. People continued to remain healthy and live longer lives, but certain diseases started to reappear: viruses and bacterial infections, some of which were strangely different from old Earth. It was as if the nanorobots weren't programmed to deal with these new invasive infections.

Dr. Burns had no logical explanation, but he surmised that, in a few hundred years, the nanorobots would be totally extinct, unless someone came along who really understood how they worked, or was able to invent something far superior. He also explained that each new generation would have fewer, if any nanorobots, adopted from the mother before birth. Consequently, human life would gradually return to its normal expectancy of up to a hundred years. They had already witnessed the passing of several multi-centenarians as their nanorobots ceased to function. Rose had been saddened at the passing of her mentor, Amadeus. He had certainly lived a lot longer than the thirty-five years recorded in the history texts of Earth. And he had left behind a marvellous repertoire for future generations to marvel and enjoy.

"I do miss him," Rose spoke somberly as she joined her husband on the castle patio, after spending most of the morning pouring out her soul on the piano, playing Amadeus' recent piano sonata. It was unfinished; he had died before it was complete. But she could well imagine the direction it was going.

"I enjoyed the music," Fred greeted her warmly, pulling her into his arms. The children were asleep in the nursery and even their unborn child appeared to have settled for the night.

"We have done it," she exclaimed, snuggling into the comfort of his arms.

"Perhaps," the king grasped her hand in his. "At least for now things are peaceful. A real oasis."

"A Garden of Eden, like the President said," she mused out loud. She snuggled closer, glancing fondly up at her husband of ten years.

Fred returned the fond gaze, adding, "And we did send a lot of our people out into the world with the blessing to…" Rose joined him in the quote, "go forth and multiply."

About The Author

Emily-Jane Hills Orford

Emily-Jane Hills Orford has fond memories and lots of stories that evolved from a childhood growing up in a haunted Victorian mansion. Told she had a 'vivid imagination', the author used this talent to create stories in her head to pass tedious hours while sick, waiting in a doctor's office, listening to a teacher drone on about something she already knew, or enduring the long, stuffy family car rides. The author lived her stories in her head, allowing her imagination to lead her into a different world, one of her own making. As the author grew up, these stories, imaginings and fantasies took to the written form and, over the years, she developed a reputation for telling a good story. Emily-Jane can now boast that she is an award-winning author of several books, including *The Piccadilly Street Series* (Tell-Tale Publishing 2018 and on), *Queen Mary's Daughter* (Clean Reads 2018), *Gerlinda* (CFA 2016) which received an Honorable Mention in the 2016 Readers' Favorite Book Awards, *To Be a Duke* (CFA 2014) which was named Finalist and Silver Medalist in the 2015 Next Generation Indie Book Awards and received an Honorable Mention in the 2015 Readers' Favorite Book Awards and several other books. A retired teacher of music and creative writing, she writes about the extraordinary in life and the fantasies of dreams combined with memories.

For more information on the author, check out her website at: http://emilyjanebooks.ca